ONE CHANCE

Steve May: a teacher, prize-winning poet, radio dramatist, jazz pianist . . . and one of the most exciting writers on the Egmont list. Every book of his is a thunderbolt, breathtaking in the quality of its writing. *One Chance* is no exception: Steve has written the ultimate classic wartime adventure story, fit to rival the storytelling of Morpurgo.

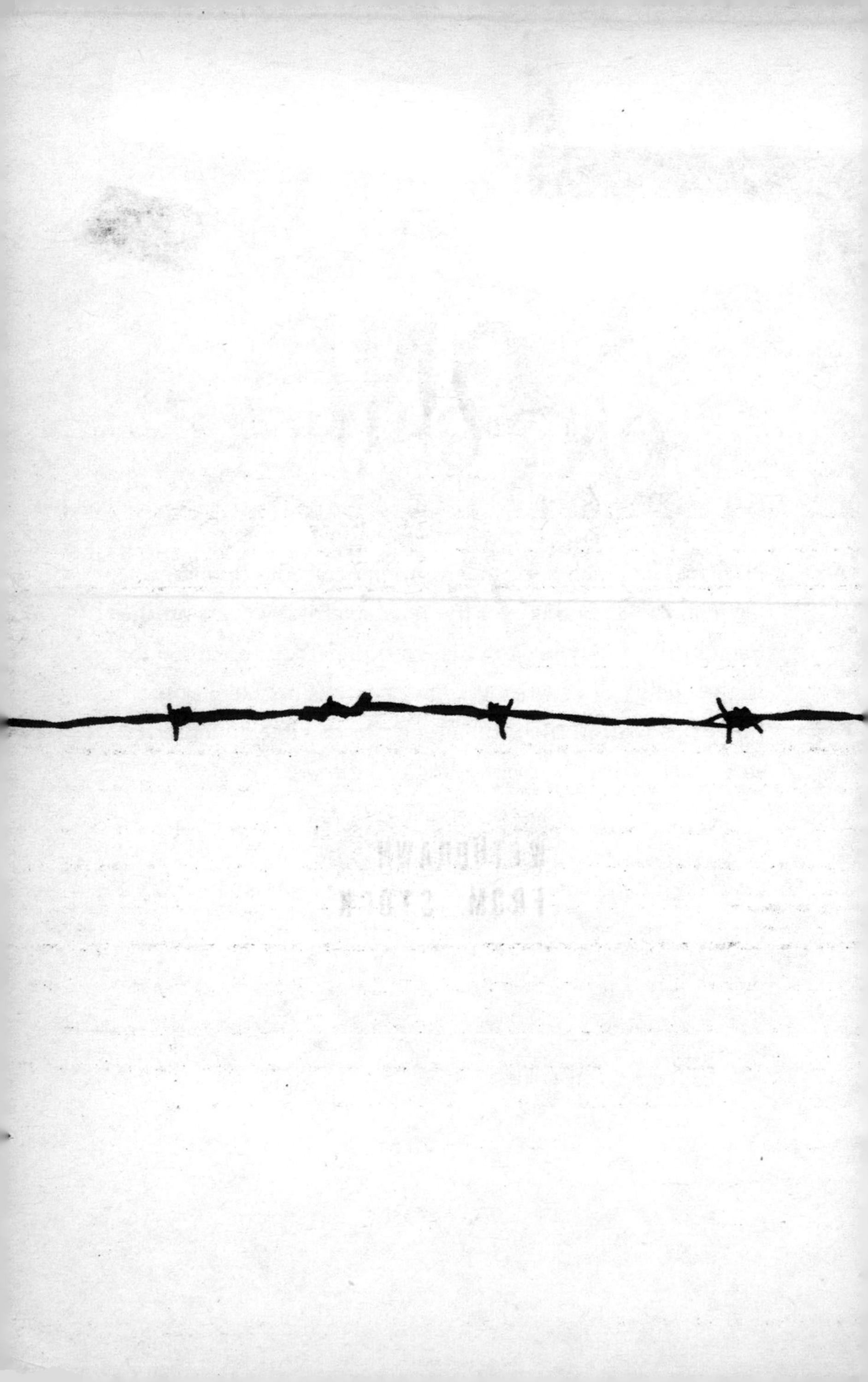

ONE CHANCE

STEVE MAY

EGMONT

With thanks to the Princess of the Catacombs.

EGMONT

We bring stories to life

First published in Great Britain 2004
by Egmont Books Limited
239 Kensington High Street, London W8 6SA

ISBN 1 4052 1626 3

1 3 5 7 9 10 8 6 4 2

A CIP catalogue record for this title is available from the British Library

Typeset by Avon DataSet Ltd, Bidford on Avon B50 4JH
Printed and bound in Great Britain by the CPI Group

Prologue

Northern France, May 1940

Flat fields, a forest, green in the sunshine. Jaq crouches at the edge of the trees, watchful, listening. Round his neck is slung a khaki bag.

The trees rustle, then shake.

Jaq straightens, alert like a hare.

There's clanking, whirring.

Jaq hugs the khaki bag to his chest, and sprawls his way into a hollow.

There's cracking and tearing, and the hot stench of diesel. The nearest trees shudder, then splinter. Above the boy's head, out pokes a pipe, a barrel; it swivels, rises, then plunges down in a mess of torn branches.

All along the rim of the forest the tanks crash out of the trees, hesitate, then with a higher whine of their engines set off across the open fields.

Chapter One

Southern France, two weeks later

Lise hesitated outside the door of Papa's study. Inside, she could hear the news voice on the wireless. Scary, droning. Armies and plans and offensives.

Lise knocked lightly, and pushed the door open.

Papa looked up quickly, and switched the radio off.

'Bang! Bang! You're dead!'

Outside, Robert is giggling, while big, red-faced Raymond, the boy from the next farm, pretend-strangles him.

Lise looks away, sits on the chair across the desk from her father.

The study was cool, and smelt of books and files and tedious brown envelopes. Papa was writing in a hardbacked accounts book. His handwriting was spidery neat. As he wrote, he frowned.

'Well?' he said, without looking up.

'I wondered, what's the news about the war?'

War. The word scares Lise in her stomach.

Papa tapped his pen. 'You know what my aunt says. I shouldn't scare you children.'

'I'd rather be scared and know what's going on.'

Her father looked at her for a moment, then nodded. 'Very well. The Germans have attacked in several places. Our armies are trying to regroup and hold them back.'

Lise pushed a big paperclip round the desk with her finger. She shivered. 'What if our soldiers don't hold them back?'

He hesitated. 'I'm sure they will.'

'And we're safe here, aren't we?'

Papa slapped the ledger shut. 'Have you walked Malcio yet today?'

Chapter Two

Jaq ran towards the bridge.

Round his neck, the khaki bag.

Silence.

Two soldiers lumbered out of the trees.

'Stop!'

Jaq put his head down and ran faster.

One of the soldiers raised his rifle, but the other grabbed his arm, and pointed into the sky. Black dots.

'Planes. Germans.'

The soldiers threw themselves into the ditch by the side of the road.

Under Jaq's bare feet, the metal of the bridge clanged.

Above, the rumble turned to a roar.

The bridge shuddered.

Jaq glanced back.

Behind him, a column of smoke and dust spurted up out of the woods, and a moment later came the crash of the explosion.

Then another, and another. A line of explosions heading for the bridge, and him.

He urged himself forward, head bobbing.

Crash! Crash! Crash!

There was a sound like tearing cotton, then a boom, a splintering, and the bridge disintegrated, green metal flying in all directions, and clouds of dust and rust. The water spouted up with a whoosh, and then fragments of metal, clods of earth, pebbles, began to clatter and splash back down again.

The rumble of the planes faded.

The two soldiers picked themselves up, wiping at the dirt on their uniforms.

'Poor little basket,' said one.

'Yeah,' replied the other. 'Even if he did steal our dinner.'

They turned and trotted back into the woods.

The spring sunshine beat down on the water and the mangled remains of the bridge. The air smelt of cordite, and smoke, and filth, and metal filings.

A dark shape bobbed near the far bank of the river. It was a head. A boy's head. The head sputtered. Jaq dragged himself out from the water, the bag still clutched under one arm. He shook himself like a dog, pulled himself up to his feet, sniffed the air, and then set off again, limping south.

Chapter Three

Malcio bounded and yapped along the road. Stones. Dust. Hot in the sun, chill in the shade. Trees. The mountain rising away. Far below, the town. Malcio snapped at everything and nothing. He wasn't a house dog, he was a work dog, but a work dog without work. He'd been left over from the previous owner of the Domaine, when the Durelles bought it two years ago. His fur was shaggy and dirty, and his eyes wild, and puzzled.

In her head, Lise is writing and rewriting a letter to her best friend, Hélène, far away in Lyon:

'I miss you so much, I wish you were here.

They call it the joke war, just because there's no fighting yet. But it's no joke for me.

I get shivery thinking about it.

It's like a shadow over everything.

Papa, he tries to explain but you can tell, he's really worried and you only have to make a joke and he snaps at you.

What I want is someone to talk to, someone like you –'

Ahead of them, the brush rustled, and a soldier loped out, and paused in the centre of the road.

Lise stopped walking.

Malcio cowered against her legs, his fur bristling.

The soldier looked past her, then waved into the woods. A line of soldiers emerged from the trees, crossed the road, and disappeared on the other side. Blue uniforms, rounded helmets. French soldiers. Ours. Chausseurs Alpins. The one in the road, she knows him; she knows all of them, they've been stationed there for months.

The soldier grinned at her, then disappeared too.

The road was empty again, ordinary.

Malcio lifted his head, and whined.

Lise breathed out at last.

Go back home?

No.

Why should she?

Potch!

Lise's stomach lurched inside her.

A rifle shot. The strange squashed echo in the valley. She took a deep breath, scanned the hillside. Someone was working their way up the slope. In and out of the bushes. Moving urgently. Carrying a large old carbine. Not a soldier.

A dumpy figure with a flat cap and a dirty overcoat and a yellow scarf at the throat. The figure stood up straight, and listened. Monsieur Pigache. Red-faced Raymond's father.

Malcio strained at the rope.

Old Pigache waved an arm, and whistled.

Another figure appeared, taller, skinnier, wearing a torn waistcoat and a crumpled brown hat. Bernard Pigache, the eldest son. He too carried his carbine. Two dogs bounded ahead of them. They disappeared into the trees. Hunting something. Some poor deer, or rabbit. Round here, they're always shooting something.

Potch!

Another shot, closer this time, and shouting. The dogs yelped, nearer and nearer, crashing through the bushes. Malcio bounced round in circles, nose to the sky, whining and snarling. Lise strained on the rope with both hands to hold him.

To the side, in the bushes, a scurrying, a scuffling.

He was on her in a moment, then past.

'*Pardon, mademoiselle.*'

A jumble of dark, cropped hair, thin face, ragged shirt, trousers, tied at the knee, bare feet. A boy, with a bag, and a chicken, limping, scampering across the road, into the bushes, and on up the Colle.

'*Pardon, mademoiselle.*'

A stranger. Dark eyes. Fourteen, fifteen years old? The shirt, torn and open at the neck. Unreal. Like a traveller from another world.

The bushes shook, and the Pigache dogs burst out, leaping and yapping. For a moment it was a chaos of paws and tails and yelps as the three dogs snarled and doubled and lunged at each other, rough and heavy against Lise's bare legs.

'Ho!'

Old Pigache stumbled up on to the roadway.

At once his dogs drew back, dragging their tails, heads lowered, as though expecting a blow.

'Did you see him?' shouted Pigache to Lise.

'Who?'

'The thief,' coughed Pigache, peering into the undergrowth. His family had farmed the hills here for generations, and he viewed incomers like Lise's family with contempt.

The trees rustled. Bernard came stooping out, grunting to himself. Lise shuddered.

Bernard was nearly thirty, but he'd never been schooled. His face was long, and bent, so front on it looked like a crescent moon. Bernard was always trying to suck his face straight, and grunting with the effort.

Monsieur Pigache hunched closer to Lise, stubble and thin lips. His voice had a sort of fluff to it. 'What's up, missy? Cat got your tongue?'

She shook her head.

'Someone,' he said slowly, as though talking to an idiot, 'someone kindly helped himself to one of our birds, and he came this way.'

Lise's heart went tight in her chest.

'A skinny son of a sow,' Pigache went on, 'with a funny scampery sort of limp, and pale as pig pudding.'

One of the dogs let out an urgent howl, and then galumphed up into the bushes. Bernard grunted and pointed.

'Found the trail,' nodded old Pigache. 'We'll have him.'

And he and Bernard hurried off up the Colle into the undergrowth. Malcio was eager to be after them, tugging and lunging.

Potch!

Potch!

The shock of the guns, so close, Lise started, loosened her grip on the rope, and Malcio was away, bounding into the trees. Lise scrambled after him.

It was gloomy, strangely silent. Malcio's rope slithered ahead of her, catching on bushes and branches and whipping up the grey dusty soil.

Suddenly, Malcio stopped, teeth bared, hackles rising, a hissing in his throat.

There was the boy, in a hollow. Crouching, stock still. The eyes fixed her. Dark big eyes, watchful, and scared and sharp. He had the bag, and the chicken, hugged to his chest.

Malcio hesitated, jerking forward, cringing back, as though held by some invisible force.

Lise could hear the Pigaches' heavy boots clumping and slithering along the slope, and the panting and yelping of the dogs.

'What's your dog found?' shouted Pigache.

The boy's dark eyes widened. Pleading. He shook his head, once. Lise's heart was icy cold.

'It's nothing – a rabbit hole,' she shouted back. And then she sank her fingers under Malcio's collar, and with a big effort she wrenched him round and hauled him along the slope, away from the boy. Malcio fought against her. His paws slipped and scrabbled on the dusty soil.

Pigache panted through the trees. His small eyes were wide and bright.

'Keep your eyes open. He can't be far.'

He pushed past her and put a hand to his mouth and hallooed. A halloo came back from further up the hill.

On the ridge stood Raymond, and next to him Lise's brother, Robert. Robert's eyes were bright with excitement. In his two hands he held an old carbine.

'Surrounded!' laughed Pigache, cocking his gun.

'You can't shoot him,' Lise said, sick in her throat.

Suddenly the dogs set off through the undergrowth, straight towards the hollow.

'No need for shooting,' grinned Pigache.

There was a growling and a snapping and a tearing. Lise could see the head of one of the dogs, shaking backwards and forwards, ripping.

'No!' she screamed.

Raymond and Robert came leaping, stumbling down through the undergrowth, cheering and hallooing.

'Got him! Got the beggar!'

Bernard clambered in among the dogs, reached down and picked up something. It was bloody. Lise shut her eyes. Old

Pigache hurried to his son.

Bernard, puzzled, shook the bloody thing.

Pigache frowned, then nodded, then spat. 'The little beggar,' he said. 'Fooled the dogs with our own bird.'

Chapter Four

Family supper. Big dark oak table.

Knives, forks: clack, silence, clack. Slow eating. Making the most of the little food they've got.

'A thief, you say?' Grande Tante frowned at Robert.

Lise bit her lip.

Excited, the words tumbled out of Robert's mouth. 'This dirty thief stole a chicken and God knows what from old man Pigache –'

Maman glanced at her son.

'Oh, all right,' corrected Robert. 'Nice Monsieur Pigache, and I helped them look for the thief, and then she came along and helped the little dishrag get away.'

Lottie pushed a fatty gob of meat round her plate. 'Raymond Pigache stinks.'

Everyone ignored her.

Grande Tante squinted at Lise. 'You helped a thief escape?'

Lise swallowed, forced herself to be calm. 'It's true I saw

a boy –' she felt her face flushing as she said the word, 'but only in the distance, I didn't know they were after him, Monsieur Pigache and his sons –'

'And me!' interrupted Robert.

'Yes, and Robert, and they asked if I'd seen him, and –' she swallowed at the hard, painful lump in her throat, eyes stinging, 'and I didn't realise he was the one they meant.'

Robert banged his knife down triumphantly. 'Old Pigache asked if she'd seen him, and she said no!'

Her father looked away.

Grande Tante made one of her stupid, big faces. 'So, you lied?'

Lise gave a little shake of the head. 'No.'

'She did! She's in love with him!' crowed Robert.

Lise struggled to keep her voice calm. 'When they said "thief" I thought of someone older – I thought they'd kill him.'

Grande Tante snorted. 'Proverb: if a girl gives two reasons neither is sufficient.'

Yvette Durelle touched Lise's hand. 'What happened next?'

'Monsieur Pigache set his dogs on him, but the boy escaped.'

Robert made a silly face. '*The boy, the boy, the lovely boy!*'

Lise turned on him. 'And you had a gun, and you would have fired it if you had the chance.'

Silence.

'What was he like?' asked Yvette.

Lise flushed again. 'About Robert's age, or younger.'

Robert made a face at her.

'Local, was he? Surely not?' said Grande Tante.

'Oh, he was an outsider, that's for sure,' Robert nodded, eagerly. 'Old Pigache reckons, probably another dirty Jew come over the mountain or some such.'

Maman glanced at her son again. 'Please, don't use that kind of language.'

Robert reared his head. 'That's what Pigache calls them. He should know. He's a proper farmer.'

Grande Tante patted his hand. 'Yvette, don't be so hard on the boy.'

Maman flushed.

Georges Durelle looked up from his plate. He'd been staring at it for some moments. He turned to Robert. 'Is it true you had a gun?'

Robert looked down at the table. 'It was only an old carbine; I was carrying it for Raymond.'

Georges Durelle took a breath. 'You know our agreement about guns.'

Robert stared down at the table. 'That's your agreement, not mine. Why do I have to be like you? Everyone laughs at you.'

'That's their business.'

'Why don't you join up for the army?'

Yvette patted her son's hand. 'Because he's too old.'

Georges carefully arranged his knife and fork on his plate. 'That's not the reason.'

'What is it then?' demanded Robert.

Georges's face paled. 'I am not prepared to discuss that with you.'

Robert raised his face, defiant. 'I wish I had a dad like Louis Beaumont, with a revolver and a uniform.'

'Please,' said Maman, taking his arm, 'stop now.'

Robert tore his arm free, and spat, 'but it's true.'

Lise's face was burning. *Yes, yes, it's true. How ashamed she was, to be ashamed of her father.*

Lottie raised her fork importantly. 'But Papa has got a gun.'

They all looked at her.

Grande Tante slapped her knife down. 'He certainly has, but he won't use it.'

Georges spoke softly. 'Please, say no more.'

Lottie lowered her eyes to the table.

Grande Tante tutted, but kept quiet.

Silence.

'Listen!' exclaimed Lottie.

'You keep out of it!' snarled Robert.

But Maman tilted her head and pushed back her hair. 'Yes, what is that noise?'

So they all listened.

'There!' said Lottie, triumphant.

A kind of baying? Echoing in the valley, but also muffled by the contours of the Colle.

'That's the Pigaches,' said Robert proudly. 'Still after him.

They shout to each other in a sort of huntsman's code.'

Yvette glanced to her husband. He looked away.

They all listened again.

The halloos drifted on the air, disembodied, like the groans of ghosts. There was the muffled *potch* of a carbine, then more shouts.

Maman lay down her napkin.

'Where do you think they are?' asked Lottie. 'Close?'

'They sound close,' agreed Maman, with a shudder. 'As if they're on our land.'

'What if they are?' demanded Grande Tante.

'Country people, they have their own ways,' said Georges, taking a sip of wine.

'What?' demanded Lise, 'they shoot people for nothing at all?'

'Best remedy for a thief,' said Grande Tante.

Maman caught her husband's eye.

Papa threw down his napkin. 'Of course, if some injustice is being done, we can't stand by and do nothing, but in this case, we know nothing of the facts. And we do have our own concerns.'

His wife wiped her mouth, and got up. 'I'll go.'

Monsieur threw down his fork, rose to his feet. 'All right, Yvette. Finish your meal.'

'Deary, deary me,' Grande Tante sighed. 'If you ask me, you folks should never have left the town.'

Chapter Five

'I'm getting hungry, Pa,' said Raymond, belching. The air was cooling, the light fading fast. 'We've been going round in circles for hours.'

'Just a little further,' insisted old Pigache, hurrying on at a stumble along the steep slope.

Ahead, Bernard sniffed and peered, dragging the exhausted dogs on a rope now.

'We're on the Durelle's land,' complained Raymond. 'You can see the lights from the house.'

'You big soft pair of knickers. It's hot pursuit. We can chase the little devil where we like.'

The slope steeper, steeper. The dry grass scratched at Jaq's knees, his thighs, his arms. Steeper and steeper, his feet slithering on the dry, dusty soil, the warm grass catching and scratching, the bag heavy under his arm, dragging him back, legs so tired, can hardly breathe.

Keep in the trees. Dark soon.

Behind him, closer and closer they're getting. Where's Italy? This way, surely?

Steeper, steeper. The dry grass scratching and pulling. The loose, dry soil crumbling. Grab the grass stems, pull yourself up the slope.

The kids' song rings in his head, over and over: 'Can't catch me, can't catch me, can't catch me.'

Watch it!

Ahead, the trees thin to nothing. A patch of earth, burnt black by a fire. Bare, exposed, in full view. Then trees again. Panting, rubbing at his arm, the boy paused.

Risk it?

Below, Bernard pointed up the hill. Old Pigache nodded, raised his carbine, licked his lips, leant against a tree, resting the barrel of the gun on a branch. Steadied himself. Raymond held his breath. Bernard watched, eyes wide, eager, nodding, grunting: 'O on, o on!'

The boy scanned he trees. Work along the cover? No. Too far. *Can't catch, can't catch me*. He tensed himself for the dash across the burnt grass.

Old Pigache waited, and waited. Above, greying in the dying light, the trees quivered, then parted. The skinny, pale figure was framed against the dark, burnt soil. Old

Pigache narrowed his eyes, and squeezed the trigger.

* * *

It seemed as though he heard the shot a fraction of a second before he felt the impact. No pain, just a shock, and suddenly he was on the ground. Dazed, he felt at his leg, at the numb lake where his leg should be, and his hand was wet with blood.

'Winged him,' snorted old Pigache, peering into the gloom up the slope.

'Finish him off!' urged Raymond.

'O on!' urged Bernard.

Pigache aimed the carbine again.

'Good evening!' called Georges Durelle, stumbling along the path from the house. Old Pigache glanced round, then back up the slope.

The boy had vanished.

Chapter Six

Lise sat in the window seat, next to her old doll's house, peering out into the dark. On the dresser her father's plate still sat, the gravy congealed to fat.'A fine meal our Georges will make tonight,' observed Grande Tante, creaking on her rocker, needles clacking.

Potch!

Grande Tante did an exaggerated jump in her chair. 'That was close!'

Robert grinned at Lise as he passed, made a throat-slit gesture. 'They'll kill the little so-and-so now, for sure.'

Lottie sidled up to Lise. 'Play a game?'

'No!'

Lottie touched the roof of the doll's house. 'Can I play with –'

'No!'

Lise got up.

'Best stay indoors now.'

'Yes, Grande Tante, I'm going to my room.'

But instead of going upstairs, Lise carried on along the hall, and slipped outside. Nearly dark now. She ducked under the lean-to where the rusted-up circular saw sat. Her place. Private. Not even Lottie dared come here. The old table, broken chair, the old lavender cushion, the cupboard, with the pretend tins, where Lise played house.

Or used to.

The hot, soft wind gusted, the house creaked like a ship in a swell.

Lise's thoughts were flurrying, so, to settle herself, she started up a story in her head for Hélène; Hélène with the wide eyes, the warm heart, the trusting nature. Hélène, who believes anything.

The Germans are attacking, and clods like Pigache try and fight, but they get scared and run away, only Papa stands firm. He stands calmly in the doorway, unarmed, and says in a quiet, firm voice to the German soldiers. 'I'm here. You'll have to get past me.' And then he takes them prisoner, and the real army arrives, and they take all the Germans away, and they say, 'Well done, Monsieur Durelle, you showed these clods how it should be done.' And that's the end of the war.

Potch! Another shot.

A face snaps into her head.

The boy.

The pale face, the dark eyes.

Uncomfortable, like an unwelcome truth, a stone in the

shoe. The dry air prickles at her cheek. Irritably, she scratches at her own face. Truth-spiders, crawling. *Why feel guilty?* Because, it's all messy: she's lied, and Papa guessed, and Grande Tante making fun, and worst of all Maman, *understanding*.

And the boy, out there somewhere, wounded? Dead?

The eyes stared at her.

She hadn't helped him, hadn't told.

Why should she care?

Why did he have to come here?

'It's hot pursuit,' blustered Old Pigache.

'You can't stop us,' jeered Raymond.

Georges Durelle stood firm on the path. 'I don't want to stop you; I want to help you.'

'We don't need help from the likes of you,' scoffed Raymond.

Old Pigache raised a hand. 'Manners, son. Neighbours should always be grateful for a bit of help, however small. Now . . .' he put on a pretend-posh voice 'shall we pursue the vagabond?'

'Of course,' said Georges Durelle uncomfortably, 'but there is one thing I must insist.'

Pigache narrowed his eyes. 'What?'

Georges hesitated. 'That you don't use firearms while you're on this property.'

'How you going to stop us?' brayed Raymond.

Again Pigache motioned his son silent. 'May I ask what you're worried about, Monsieur Durelle?'

Georges Durelle met his eye. 'Theft is one thing, murder is another.'

Old Pigache nodded. 'Far be it from me to trespass against my neighbour's wish.' He cracked open his carbine and slid out the cartridges.

'Thank you,' said Georges.

'Don't thank me, Monsieur, thank the good manners of the local area. It's the way we all get along with each other, live and let live. And we stand up for each other, and we don't let our neighbours down, even if they are a bit cracked in the head department.' He slung the carbine over his shoulder with the barrel pointing down. 'And if we meet a rogue with a gun and we're all killed, you can feel as holy as you like.' He paused. 'Have you sold your lemons yet?'

Georges Durelle shook his head.

'Well,' grinned Pigache nastily, 'I wish you the very best of luck.'

Stumbling on, stumbling on, *can't catch, can't catch.* Blood – always seems more than there really is.

The boy slumped down, trying to think. Pain gnawing in on the wound.

He gasps.

His head jerks round.

Dark in the fading light, the patchy trail of his own blood on the grey soil.

Leans on a tree, hanging, rips and tugs at his shirt. Half the front comes away in tatters. Rolls it, hasty, then winds it anyhow round the thigh, pulls it tight, tighter so it seems to squeeze the pain, will burst it, but it won't burst, it grows and grows, and swells and swells.

He ties the knot.

Got to hide, got to hide.

Peers round, in the gloom, the trees, it's all blurring.

What's that ahead?

As they tramped up the slope, puffing, Old Pigache explained.

'Thanks to the chicken, he gave us the slip on the Colle, but we followed his trail down – then we lost him again at the river, but we split both ways, and Bernard here nosed him out, and we caught up with him on the ridge.'

'Look!' called Raymond, squatting, fingering the brown, stained dust.

'It looks like blood,' said Georges Durelle.

'Bang!' grunted Bernard, miming a recoil.

'Come on,' nodded Pigache. 'We're nearly on him.'

Lise started. Voices. Boots. Hurrying.

She stood up, not breathing.

Cold air fanned her face. What's that? A smell, a sour,

slimy smell like old mud – and then the fingers clasped round her mouth. A thin bony hand, each finger alive like an eel. The hand smelt of scum, mud, rotten grass.

His face was right up close to hers.

The boy.

He was hanging on to her, his fingers digging into her flesh.

'Don't scream,' he hissed. 'Won't hurt you.'

She let out a grunt of surprise, and jerked away.

He stumbled, his foot slipping from under him, grasped her again, and automatically she held him under one arm. Her hands were on his flesh, the bony body smeared with muck and slime, dragging down on her. Under his other arm, the bag, clutched.

And bandaged in a mess of cloth, red blood, brown blood, his leg. The smell caught in her throat. She let go of him, stepped back, retching. He sprawled on to the flagstones, a grey shape, writhing like a worm in the gloom by the workbench.

In here! My place!

She pressed back against the wall, her mouth open. She was still panting out a kind of 'no' sound.

The white of his face owled up at her. The thin lips moved. 'I was right,' he whispered.

'What?'

'You are an angel.'

Chapter Seven

The men and dogs came swarming up the slope and into the yard. Yvette Durelle stood on the porch step. 'Have you found him?'

'Not yet,' puffed Georges.

'We're pretty warm, ma'am,' shouted Old Pigache.

Yvette stepped down into the yard. The dogs drew back. 'So you think he's here?'

Bernard nodded, vigorously, not to her, but to his father.

'For certain,' said Old Pigache.

Malcio snarled in the dog barn.

'Have a look?' asked Pigache.

'Of course.' Georges flipped the big latch, and dragged the door open. Malcio howled.

'Huh,' said Old Pigache gruffly, 'that's a mad one if ever there was.'

Bernard poked his head in the door, Papa shone a light.

There was a yap and a scurry, and Bernard quickly snapped his head back.

'If the thug hides in there, he'll get his bum well bitten,' said Raymond.

'Better have a proper look,' insisted old Pigache.

Bernard nodded to Raymond, and grunted.

'I wish I had a little brother,' grumbled Raymond, 'I'd make sure he did all the dirty work.'

He took a step into the barn.

Malcio yapped, howled, and then the howl shrank to a whimper.

Grande Tante emerged from the house, wrapping her shawl round her big shoulders. 'Monsieur Pigache, a thief's a thief, but this is a lot of trouble for one chicken.'

'Madame Dubosson, it's not just a chicken,' retorted Pigache. 'If it was just a scrawny hen the little basket took, I'd be home in bed and all forgotten.' He paused, and leaned on his carbine. 'The thing is, he's been in our house.'

'And taken something?' demanded Grande Tante.

Pigache took a deep breath. His voice was hoarse, almost like a child about to cry. 'He's had away my poor wife's crucifix, God bless her. It hung in our best parlour since we was wed, and not a cheap one, let me tell you, proper oak the wood and Our Lord, God rest him, figured in solid brass. Not a trinket we're talking of here, and we always leave our doors unlocked, I reckon you do too, being neighbours, and knowing each other, and trusting each other, and now it's gone.' He stared at Madame Durelle's throat. 'And the thing is, that's not a chicken, that's not a bird, you don't eat that kind of thing however hungry you are. You take it if you're a thief, for the metal in it, to melt it down and sell to tinkers.'

He choked on the last word.

Yvette nodded. 'I understand your feelings, Monsieur Pigache –'

'I'm not sure you do, not coming from the neighbourhood, and big city types to boot, beg your pardon.'

Raymond stepped out of the barn. 'No sign.'

Bernard grunted, and lifted his crescent face to the sky, twitching his nose, twisting his mouth.

'Have you lost the scent?' demanded old Pigache.

Bernard shrugged, grunted.

One of the dogs nosed at some steps.

Old Pigache's eyes were quick. 'What's down there?'

'A sort of den,' explained Yvette. 'Where the children play.'

'Mind if we take a lookey?'

'By all means.'

Bernard and Raymond dragged the dogs down the short slope.

A moment later, the dogs are yapping and howling. Raymond bellows up, 'Come on, Dad, we've caught the trail again.'

In the fading light, Lise has the boy under the arm, they're scuttle-scurrying a strange, three-legged race, along the lemon grove, round the corner by the warrior palms, then down the steps, alongside the big metal pipe, headlong down the path.

In the gloom, a concrete shape, a square.

'What's that?' he asks.

'A sort of drain.'

Her idea. The sluice. Where they're forbidden to play. Too dangerous.

'Can you make it down the ladder?'

He peers down. 'Have to. Wait.'

Gritting his teeth, in one quick movement, he tears the rag of shirt from the wounded leg. 'Take it, and run.'

Old Pigache leaned on the fat metal pipe, panting. 'One minute.'

The dogs strained on the ropes. Georges Durelle pointed down the hill. 'How about the inspection sluice.'

'Good idea,' nodded Pigache. 'Let's go.'

They picked their way across, and peered down the concrete sides into the gloom.

'I'll go down and have a look,' said Georges.

He swung himself awkwardly over the side, and thumped on down the wooden ladder. It creaked and banged under his weight.

'Anything?' called Pigache.

'Hang on.'

Georges thrust his arm into the in-pipe. 'There's something here!'

The Pigaches craned over the wall.

Georges wriggled and jerked his arm. 'Jammed,' he puffed.

Then there was a squeal and a squawk, and Georges was flung on to his backside. A dark brown shape, sleek and fat, leapt and disappeared down the out-pipe.

Bernard wheezed, Raymond brayed with laughter.

Pigache shook his head. 'You city folk, can't tell a rat from a thief!'

'Hang on,' said Raymond.

Bernard was grunting, pointing across the slope. They all turned to look. The warrior palms seemed to be dancing.

'Someone's up there!'

The dogs howled, pulled on the ropes.

'Come on,' said Pigache. 'Let's go and have a look.'

Lise rounded the barn, hauled herself up on to the coal bunker. Reached up to the sill. Yes! The window was still open. Pushed it up a fraction more, and wormed her way through. As her feet found the floor, she heard voices at the foot of the stairs.

Maman: 'If he's hurt they should keep searching.'

Grande Tante: 'Well, I for one won't sleep easy with a thief on the loose.'

Lise darted into the washroom, and wiped at the smears of mud and blood on her arms.

Footsteps on the stairs.

She kicked off her shoes, pulled the biggest towel from the shelf, and wrapped it round herself.

Maman appeared in the doorway. 'Are you OK?'

Lise yawned. 'Why shouldn't I be?'

In the sluice, something moved. Squirming out of the big inlet pipe. Jaq. Kneeling, he shook himself, then sank flat on to the concrete floor.

Hard day. Hard night to come. He tried to flex the leg. There's a numb hole where the thigh should be. The pain's there, but far away.

Don't give up now.

Strange, not hungry. Or thirsty. As though the fever in the blood has taken him over.

He hauls himself up, balancing on the good leg, clinging to the ladder. Italy, that way. Not far now. He narrows his eyes, peering up at the square of sky. Are they mountains, or clouds, looming in the dark?

There's the moon.

He picks up the bag. So heavy. Slings it round his shoulders, tries a step on to the ladder. He leans his weight on the ankle. There's a moment of agony, then it's as though the ankle disappears. The leg collapses under him, and he lands in a heap on the concrete.

From her bedroom window, Lise has stared at the barn so

long that the walls are fading and blurring. Nothing seems real tonight. She tries to piece it all together, fragments dazzling like a shattered window in a brilliant light.

'You are an angel.'

The feel of his bony body.

The mud smell.

The wound.

Flashes of words, of moments, the half-light, the boy, the weight of him. The pieces are alive, they rage about in her head like a rough sea.

His white face in the gloom, as he struggles on to the sluice ladder. The shirt-bandage blood-wet in her hand. 'Go now.' Then he'd looked at her. His thin lips on her hand, a kind of dry kiss like an insect. Then he'd glanced about, sniff. 'Where's Italy?'

She points to the mountains. 'That way, but it's steep. When are you going?'

'By morning.'

And his head ducks down the shaft.

She flings the bloody rag into the stream, then worms her way back through the pine grove, back up to the house.

Now, her legs and arms sting with the memories of the scramble.

She pauses. Gathers herself. Lets her heart slow down. Thoughts are still hovering and fluttering in her head.

The bag. It had banged against her. Heavy. Hard. Metal things inside?

The thought swells up, threatens to swallow her: *What have I done?*

I helped a thief escape.

No, that's not right, because he didn't escape. He's still on our land, our farm. Like a secret, a tumour.

Lise tiptoes across the room.

'What are you doing?'

Lottie, voice thick with sleep.

'Nothing, shut up.'

Lottie sighs and rolls over.

Jaq squirmed himself into a corner, and studied his little prison. Could see it all clearly in the moonlight: the big round hole for the pipe in, and another for the big pipe out again. To the side, the green metal pump with the faded and scraped gold lettering. The mesh filter, the big round stop-cock wheel.

He huddles himself tighter into the corner. Keep warm.

All you can do is fix your mind on the next thing.

The pain beast stirs in his leg. His eyes are foggy. *Don't give up now.*

Outside, a scuffling. He tenses. The small knife clicks open, smooth in his palm. The ladder shifts, clacks on the wall. His hand tightens on the knife. *One effort, force yourself.*

As Lise stepped off the ladder, he caught her, one arm round her neck, the knife at her throat. She gasped, and struggled. For a moment he held her. *One move of his arm, and her neck's broken.* The moment, the power, the temptation, all poised like scales on the tipping point.

'Please,' she croaks.

He lets her go, and sinks back down.

'Get yourself killed,' he coughs.

She kneels by him, holds out a picnic basket. 'I brought some things.'

The boy gnawed at the bread. He gulped down the water. Shook the empty flask.

'Water's short,' she said, 'I'll bring you more when I can.'

He winced. Lise stared at the thigh. Messy.

Somewhere across the valley a cock crows.

'My name's Lise,' she said, 'what's yours?'

He breathed in and out, deeply, dark eyes, still above the chewing mouth. Eyes probing.

The trick is, how much truth to tell.

'Jaq,' he said, and coughed again. 'My name's Jaq.'

Hot. Eyes blurry. This girl, her face: so solemn, the dark brows, the wide cheeks. Food. The pain pulsing, in and out, like a big valve in a river, pulsing, not in him, somewhere else.

'I thought they'd found me,' he said. 'Some bloke came down.'

'My dad. I made a noise up the hill.'

She keeps on talking, the words double up and fall over each other in his head.

Takes a bite of sausage. *Think.*

Strange light. Dawn? Have to stay another day.

The girl, she's *still* talking. What?

'Your leg, it's very bad, I think you need a doctor.'

He grasps her wrist. 'No! No doctor.'

Her face, scared.

Don't upset her. He winces. 'It's the pain. I can't think straight.'

'Can I get something?'

He shook his head, to clear it. 'Bandages? Ointment? Blanket?'

She gets up. 'All right, I won't be long.'

He grasps her wrist again. Glares up at her. 'Don't tell.'

She shakes her wrist free, hurt. 'I won't tell.'

He looks away. She clatters up the ladder.

Chapter Eight

Maman sets up the big wooden bowl under the mangle in the yard.

Lise is very helpful. Helps get breakfast ready while Robert milks the cows. Now clears away. Everything she does, normal. Except, she's watching herself, watching her hands cut the bread, watching her feet pad across the wooden floor. As though she's a ghost of herself, come from a strange world.

'You're quiet,' observes Maman. Holds up a sheet, and tuts. 'Full of holes.'

'Maman –'

'Yes?'

'Could I have that?'

'What for?'

Lise flushes. 'To play, in my den.'

Maman looks the sheet over. 'I don't suppose it's worth mending. Here.'

Lise takes the sheet, bunches it up, walks away.

Maman calls, 'Where are you going?'

'Not far. Just to the olive groves.'

'Be careful.'

Among the olive trees, a man was working, a short, swarthy man in a white smock shirt. His hair was grey white, and messy, curly.

'Hello, Giuseppe,' Lise said.

The man glanced up. His eyes were dark brown, keen. 'What?'

'I was wondering if you could help me.'

He straightened up, suspicious. 'How?'

'It's a project we're doing at school.'

He spat. 'I hate school.'

'To do with traditional remedies.'

The sheet ripped easily. Lise laid the strips out neatly in front of her on the concrete floor. Frowning with concentration, she opened the small jar Giuseppe had given her. The air was filled with a fresh, tingling fragrance, like mint mixed with pine.

Jaq sniffed. 'What's that?'

'Ointment.' Lise dipped a rag into the jar. 'It's for animals, but it's better than nothing.'

Lise moved the cloth towards the wound. Hesitated.

Parts of the wound were dark, oozing fresh blood. Other

parts had green pus and yellow slime. In places a crust had formed. There was dirt, and grass matted in with the blood.

'It needs washing.'

'Just wrap it up.' Jaq squirms on the concrete, resting back on his elbows.

'We've got to do it properly.'

'If you mess with it,' through clenched teeth, trying to keep the anger out, 'it's going to start bleeding and I'll bleed to death.' Tries to soften his voice. 'Just patch me up, that's all I need.'

He blinked. The girl, the world, everything was pulsing in and out, backwards and forwards, and slanting, off to the left. He shook his head.

She's staring at his leg with her serious eyes.

'Do it!' he urges.

And she reaches down with the rag and dabs at the wound.

Jaq squirms, jumps, almost screams in a whisper. 'For God's sake, don't pussyfoot. Do it hard, like you mean it.'

As she worked, the question loomed and floated in her head. The longer she delayed, the more impossible to say the words. *About the crucifix.*

She finished the bandage. It looked very white and clean, so long as you didn't think about what was under it.

Jaq yawned. He closed his eyes and rested his temple on the cold concrete floor. *Go away, go away, go away.*

She stood up.

'There's one thing,' she said.

He grunted.

'You took that chicken, didn't you?'

He grunted, yes, again.

'Did you take anything else?'

His eyes flicked open. 'Like what?'

Lise felt her neck flushing. 'Monsieur Pigache says he lost a crucifix too.'

'You think I took it?'

'No, I'm just asking.'

'Does it matter, if I did?'

She hesitated. 'No.'

'But you think I took it.'

'No, but your bag, it's very heavy.'

'Very heavy.'

Silence.

'I just wondered, if someone did take a crucifix, if it was because they wanted, you know, some kind of help?'

She reached in her pocket. 'I brought you this.'

In her hand, she held out a bundle of beads. A *rosary*.

He looked at it. Things were fading, going milky. He forced himself up on his elbow. 'You want to know what's in the bag?'

She shook her head.

He dragged himself closer to her, so she could smell his breath. His eyes flickered like candles, sharp, dull, sharp, dull. With his hand, he knocked the rosary on to the floor.

'I don't need your help, or God or anyone. What do I

want with a crucithing? He reached behind him and dragged the bag rasping across the floor. 'I'll tell you what's in here. My ma's things, her last things.' He coughed. 'Worthless things I dug in the rubble with my bare hands, after the bombs dropped. A candlestick, a flat iron, I don't know.' He gestures carelessly. 'Junk. I haven't looked since I put it in there. I can't face it. But you, go on, if you're so interested, get it all out and have a good look at it.'

He pushed the bag towards her.

She's shaking her head. 'No, I couldn't. I wouldn't, I only wanted to hear you say it yourself.'

He reached forward and took her hand. 'Lise.' It's the first time he's said her name! His eyes are glowing. 'Have you ever eaten a rat?'

She shook her head.

'Well I have, and a bit of a cat. And I've been shot at and chased and I've slept in a hedge, and in doorways, I've had drunken men wee on me in the night, and I've been so cold I tipped out the rubbish from a bin and burrowed into it, and I stole a chicken, yes, and once I stole a shirt off a line because I was so cold at night, but, Lise, I swear to you on my mother's grave, on my mother's corpse in the street where I found it, I have never seen, or touched, or taken any crucifix.' Then he let go of her hand and lay back, panting. 'Anyone who did that, they'd be cursed.'

He crossed himself. His eyes were bright, proud. He coughed, and the phlegm rattled in his throat.

Lise's heart was all fizzy, the air was fizzy. She needed to say something, but all she could say was, 'I knew it.'

He felt carefully in the bag. Slid something out.

'What's that?' Lise asked.

She leaned over, trying to see. What? A crumpled piece of card? With a picture on it? His hand was half open, the card resting on the fingers.

'Have a look,' he said.

She picked up the card. It was the lid from a box, the kind of box you get from a cake shop. The picture was of a chalet kind of house, with trees, a lake, and a snow-capped mountain in the background. A boy and a girl were dancing in front of the house, and a goat, and they were all smiling.

'That's where I'm going,' he said.

She looked again at the picture. 'Where is it?'

He closed his eyes. 'Can't you read?'

She spelt out the words above the picture: '*Confiserie Suisse*.'

'That means Switzerland, doesn't it?' he asked.

She nodded.

'Well,' he said, 'that's where I'm going, that's the plan. Cos Switzerland, it's clean, it's pretty, and they don't fight wars.'

He sighed, and shuddered, and his body twitched.

She handed the card back. He took it carelessly, as though it meant nothing to him.

'Switzerland,' she said. 'I've never been there.'

'Well,' he said, 'it's near Italy. You've got to go through Italy to get there. Italy's my next stop.'

Lise nodded. She was thinking of the boy and the girl dancing in the picture.

Jaq slipped the card inside the tatters of his shirt.

'I bet you dance,' he whispered.

She swallowed. 'Only at school.'

In bed, Lise tried to calm her racing heart with fantasies of eating rats and cats in back streets with fires made of furniture. Drunken men stumbled, bombs crashed down, everything was wet with rain – but it all had a joy, a glow about it, because she was with Jaq. She pretended they were living together on the streets, making do and keeping warm, hiding, begging, stealing – and there was no doubt about it: it was the best life you could live.

Chapter Nine

Lise hesitated at the school gate.

Girls are rushing everywhere, squealing and screaming and shoving.

Lottie squeezed Lise's hand. 'What are they playing?'

Isabel Echamel has a bundle, a raggy bundle, and she's chasing, rushing, here, there, trying to catch someone, anyone, but the other girls dodge away, squealing and jeering.

They're chanting something. 'Thief! Thief! Thief!'

Marie Trevette points towards Lise. 'It's Lise the louse.'

'She saw the thief!'

'She helped him!'

The girls press round in a circle. Lottie presses against Lise's legs.

Marie stands right in front of Lise. 'What was he like?'

Lise shakes her head. 'I only caught a glimpse.'

The other girls crow, chorus it, trying to imitate Lise's accent. 'Caught a glimpse! Caught a glimpse!'

Isabel Echamel holds out the bundle. 'She ought to be the thief.'

'That's right!' the others chorus.

Lottie frowns, looking up at their faces.

'I'm sorry,' Lise says, 'but I'm not playing.' She tries to push on through the circle.

'You've got to play,' shouts Marie, pulling at her arm. And they've got her, hard fingers on her arms, pulling her, pushing her. She loses Lottie's hand, the girls push in and now with a jarring thump she's on the ground, held. Isabel is sitting on top of her, pinning her down, and now the raggy bundle, someone's pressing it into her face, rubbing it, smearing it, cold and wet and mildew.

'Thief! Thief! Thief!'

Assembly. Madame Hibou. Short and stout. White collar starched to the throat. Big brooch, arrow-shaped. Silver hair helmet, casket cut, fair skin, red cheeks, gold glasses perched on a button nose. Trying to keep her small mouth stern. The wart on her cheek dances. She looks down her nose at the paper, then up over the glasses.

'Girls. I have news. According to our government, the situation is serious, but not grave. The Germans have attacked all along our front. Our army is holding its own, and in many places pushing the Germans back.'

Lise couldn't wait till after supper. As soon as they had eaten, she set off for the sluice. Bubbling. With what? Good news. We're winning the war. Marie Trevette hates her, so what? In her pocket, tightly folded, is the page torn out of the school atlas: 'Northern Italy and Switzerland.'

Maybe he's got better. Maybe he's got so much better he's gone.

She clattered down the ladder. Stopped.

He was lying strangely, in the gloom under the overhang. As though some bird had beaked him up and dropped him, so his arms and legs lay twisted, anyhow.

His head lolled.

Lise edged closer, squatted down.

Breathing? Yes. A sort of sob, a choked sob.

Lise waited, listening, counting the seconds between each gasp.

He coughed, as though choking. His eyes slit open a fraction.

He stood inside his own head, like a lizard in a cave. He could see out of his own nose. The cave was long and winding, and he was running down it. Everything muddled together: the numb pain in his thigh, the smell of the sluice, the face of the farmer, the feel of the dead chicken. The dog. And here, this girl, with the serious face, like an angel in a painting.

His lips move. 'Drink?'

She startles.

'I thought you might be dead.'

'Not yet.'

Lise ran up the slope to the tank. Dipped in the ladle. It scraped on the bottom. Carefully she eased it out, and poured the precious liquid into the toy flask.

Jaq tried to prop himself up against the wall.

Daylight? Losing track of time. He struggles to move, but it's as though he's wrapped in sticky spider's threads. *The girl, she's at the wrong end of a telescope, fading, tiny, holding out a cup*. Try and tell her, get me out, throw me a rope, but the ship glides under the water, and there's nothing, only the blackness filling him up like water filling a jug.

Lise pushes the cup to his lips, but the lips are stiff.

Silence.

Light fading.

It's not right.

She counts his breaths, waiting for the rattle in the throat. She knows the shape of his head now. It's a thin head, but with a kind of bulge at the back, behind the ears. Some angles, he's handsome, strong-featured, but if he rolls the other way the chin is a bit weak-looking – like a guilty person answering an accusation. *Nineteen, twenty, twenty-one – go on!*

His head jerks, the breath rattles in his throat, Lise counts again. *Three, four, five, six*, holding her own breath with the effort of listening.

What if he dies? Twenty-one, twenty-two, twenty-three, it's your fault, twenty-seven, twenty-eight.

Lise glances down at the new bandage. Already there are brown and yellow stains oozing up from underneath.

Can't be right, thirty-three, thirty-four –

She edges closer, in case she misses – what's that? A vague white cloud, oozing up like a ghost round his head?

Lise pushes his shoulder, so his head flops round, heavy head, and there's a rattle in his throat, a loud ugly rattle. She pulls at his rag of a shirt – *what to do, what to do?* The head flops again. With her fingers she prises open the lips; the teeth are clenched. She squeezes at the sides of the jaw like with Malcio to get him take his worm pill.

Gradually the jaw slackens.

She breathes deeply, plunges her mouth down and fastens on the thin lips. Breathes her air slowly, slowly into his mouth, feels his chest stiff and thin, tries again, again, and then the chest, his chest, gives a twitch. Once more, she breathes clean air, fastens down, exhales through his thin lips, and his chest lifts like a sea wave, and he coughs, and rolls away, violently away, and he's almost on all fours, like a boxer knocked down, spluttering, shaking his head.

Then his hands slip, and he sprawls on his face, spread-eagled, one arm loose over the bag.

Lise stared at him, at the bag.

'I swear on my mother's grave, on my mother's corpse –'

She shivered.

Two thin straps, that's all, to unfasten it.

'On my mother's grave. Her last things.'

Lise stood up, looked round. There's a gap behind the pump. Clogged with mushy leaves and twigs. She lifted the heavy bag awkwardly into the recess, then scrabbled the mulch and mess of leaves over it. She stepped back. You'd never know the bag was there.

When she turned to look at Jaq again, a thin trickle of blood was running out of the corner of his mouth.

Lise ran. Struggling up the overgrown path. Slippery with the big raindrops. Up towards the warrior palms. Runs, runs. Bursts out on to the track, then left into the olive grove. Blocking her way is Giuseppe.

Yvette Durelle is patiently peeling potatoes, shucking the skins in one spiral, plopping the white vegetables into the big hissing pot. 'Grande Tante got some vegetables from the market –' she saw her daughter's face. Upped at once, wiping her hands. 'What is it?'

Lise forced the words out. 'I found the boy. He's hurt.'

Giuseppe laid the boy on the couch. Maman hesitated. 'How long has he been like this?'

Lise stared at the floor. 'I don't know.'

Bright red blood welled up from under the filthy dressings. Red blood streaked his pale face. Maman stood back. 'Go and get your father. Now.'

* * *

Georges Durelle worked fast, intent, his white shirtsleeves rolled up. 'I'll need hot water, scissors, iodine, clean rags.'

'The water's low.'

Lise said, 'I'll go.'

Ran out with the bucket, up the steps to the tank. The water clanged into the bucket, so loud. Back down the steps, into the kitchen, where the pan spat on the hob.

Lise hung in the doorway, hushed. Never seen her father like this, so intent, *so practical.* The white shirt was smeared with blood. He handled the wound firmly, but not roughly, with the firmness of someone who knows what they're doing, and what has to be done.

Giuseppe assisted, attentive, respectful. *Never seen him like that either.*

'It's bad,' Georges said. 'So far as I can tell the cartridge passed right through the flesh, no bone damage, but it's been left dirty too long.'

He teased off another layer of bandage. 'There's some kind of slimy stuff all over it.'

Lise glanced at Giuseppe.

Georges peeled off another strip of bandage. 'Bleeding again.' He sat beside the boy and leaned on the leg, applying pressure with his arm along the groin. 'I need a strap, a belt.'

Lise felt round her waist. The belt slipped off, the dress fell loose.

Georges took it without looking at her, quickly slung it under the thigh, then looped and tightened it.

'He needs a doctor,' he said.

'Drive him in the car?' suggested Yvette.

Georges shook his head. 'Can't be moved.'

'I'll go,' said Lise.

Papa ignored her.

Maman tore the old sheet into strips, passed the strips to Lise. Lise rolled them, then pinned them with a safety pin. *Waiting, for Maman to say something.*

Maman said nothing.

On the couch, the boy: the air gurgled in his throat. *Strange to see him, in the clear light, in their house.* The big clock ticked.

Useless, all your fault. So stupid, thinking she was helping him. The rosary! It makes her cringe to think of it, the bread, the slice of sausage. *And all the time he was dying.*

Maman's hand touched hers. 'It was lucky you found him.'

Lise pulled her hand away. 'Is there anything else I can do to help?'

'Sit with him, while I try and get some more water.'

Monsieur Pigache yawned, stretched and flipped his braces off his shoulders with a jerk of his thumbs. Another day done. The pot plopped on the hob. He stirred the thick, dark stew with the big, wooden spoon, licked it, frowned, banged it on the hearth.

The last of the sun struggled through the half-shuttered

kitchen window. The old man sighed, rubbed his back, hesitated by the dresser.

Between two large, browny cream photos of stern old women, was a bare patch, where the paint was much lighter, a bare patch where something had hung before, and now hung no longer, a bare patch in the shape of a cross.

Pigache frowned, looked lower: the photo of a young man in soldier's uniform stood proudly next to a tattered flag. Pigache bent down to the dresser cupboard, and pulled out a corked bottle. The dark, red liquid splashed into the tumbler. Pigache drew himself as tall as he could, then with a glance towards the tatty flag, and half a salute with his right hand, he grunted, 'Good luck, Marcel, old son, you'll need it,' and emptied the wine down his throat in one noisy gulp.

A loud knocking at the door. 'Monsieur Pigache, Monsieur Pigache!'

Pigache clacked open the fly-door.

Robert was on the step.

'What's the rush?' grumbled old Pigache. 'We're not potting rabbits tonight.'

Lise sat by the bed.

He looks like a corpse already.

She blinked. So tired. Tired of this. Too much. She yawned so wide her jaw clicked.

And then the thought formed and popped up hard as a

billiard ball: '*I wish he was dead.*'

She got up. *So gloomy in here*. Wind the wick up on the lamp. *Matches?*

And then, as if tripped by a switch, his eyes opened, and he was staring at her.

Robert crouched up on the ridge above the house, sucking the back of his hand. *Better not too close*. Excited, scared. Like when you tear the wings off a butterfly. Where are they? *There*. Pigache and his sons cross the yard like a storm. Pigache pulls open the fly-door, kicks at the front door. It swings in, and they disappear into the house.

Chapter Ten

Lise heard the door slam, ran out into the passage, tried to block the way but Pigache grasped a handful of dress, and hair, and flung her aside. She crashed into the wooden panelled wall.

Old Pigache stepped over her to the couch, ripped away the bedding with one angry movement, slapped the boy once, twice, then hauled, dragged, threw him on to the floor.

Lise glanced round. Her nose was smarting, angry. *In our house, these clodhoppers*. Raymond, Bernard, one each side, hauled the boy to his feet, so he hung between them, head lolling.

Old Pigache swung his carbine by the barrel, and the heavy wooden stock thudded into the boy's ribs. Blood and spit sprayed from his mouth.

Lise upped and flung herself, pulling at Pigache's jacket. He slapped and wafted, caught her two or three glancing blows, swung her this way and that, but she clung on. The slick corduroy reeked of garlic, tobacco, and paraffin.

Hands grasped her waist, pulling her away. Raymond. The feel of his hands on her drove Lise wild with anger. She flung her head back, and caught him flush on the nose, and with a howl he let go of her. She stumbled, lost her grip on the old man's jacket.

He pulled away, swung the carbine. Lise lunged, felt the weight of the wooden stock, her nails caught Pigache's bare arm. He swore, squared up to her, swung his free hand. The slap knocked her into a sudden humming silence. She was on the floor. He was over her, had her by the throat of her dress, raised his hand to strike again.

'Stuck-up little –'

'Excuse me.'

Maman stood in the doorway.

Pigache, stumbling, let Lise go. With his raised arm, he reached up, pulled his hat off. Yvette Durelle advanced on him.

'Excuse me,' she said, 'but I don't remember inviting you into my house. Certainly not with boots in that state, and guns on your arms. Certainly not to manhandle my children.'

She reached down, and pulled Lise to her feet. Lise's cheek and nose were still stinging. The room hummed. The dark material of Maman's dress was warm and smelt of washing and rosewater. Maman turned to Bernard, who still held the slumping boy by one arm. 'Put him on the bed, please.'

Bernard, eyes wide, mouth wide, edged clumsily across the room, half dragging the boy.

'Gently!' scolded Maman.

Pigache twisted his hat in his hands, stumbled over his words. 'The thief, it's him, no doubt, and she, the girl, she got obstreferous –'

'Thief or not, he's extremely badly hurt.'

Pigache was almost pleading: 'Madame, much as I appreciate your good intentions of the fairer sex, my Marette was just the same God rest her, but don't you see, we're going to do what we came here to do, there's nothing you can do to stop it, only make it more unpleasant – so will you please see reason and step aside?'

Maman leaned close to the boy, feeling his pulse. Her voice was calm. 'And what did you come here to do?'

Pigache's mouth twisted, as though he was torn between good manners and exasperation at this woman's stupidity. 'I tell you what,' he said, 'we'll take him out, away from your house. I know how upsetting it must be, you won't hear a thing, I promise you – and I'll make sure you get a bunch of flowers for your pains.'

Maman stood up to face him. Raymond shrank back. 'No. I would rather you produce some evidence for your accusations.'

Pigache held his ground, spoke to her neck.

'Evidence, we've plenty of.'

'Such as?'

'We saw him.'

Maman moved to the side table, gestured off-hand at a small pile of odds and ends. 'You can see exactly what he's got with him.'

Pigache picked gingerly at the heap: some string, two stones, a rag of a kerchief, the remains of the trousers, and the knife.

Maman looked up. 'Is any of that your stolen property?'

Pigache jerked his hand away from the stuff, rounded on Yvette. 'No it is not, and if you don't mind we'll have a little less of the sarcasm, which may go down well in your town drawing rooms, but here we like to speak plainer.' He raised the knife. 'For a start, we've got an offensive weapon.'

Yvette glanced at it. 'I'd call that a picnic knife.'

Bernard grunted, and made gestures round his shoulders with his hands.

Raymond nodded. 'The bag, he had a bag, remember?'

'Right enough he did,' said Pigache, nodding approvingly to his sons. He turned to Yvette Durelle. 'I don't suppose you've come across his bag? Bag this kind of size. Khaki, kind of despatch bag. Probably heavy? Full of thefted items?'

Yvette shook her head. She appealed to Lise.

Lise, mouth tight, shook her head too.

Old Pigache leaned closer to her, a leering smile on his face. 'Are you quite sure about that, young lady?'

Lise looked into his small red eyes. Nodded again.

Maman squeezed Lise's shoulders. 'Where was it you found the boy?'

Lise swallowed. 'Down the slope. Past the lemon grove. In the old shepherd's hut. You know, the one where Giuseppe keeps his tools.'

Robert looked at the back of his hand. He'd sucked it bright red. It was five, ten minutes since the commotion, the screams, the shouting. Now the house was quiet. *What on earth's going on?*

The door burst open.

Pigache marched out, flanked by his two sons.

Robert scrambled down the slope. 'Did you find him?' he called. 'What have you done to him?'

They ignored him.

Robert chased after Raymond. 'See you at scouts tonight?'

Raymond lashed out with his flat hand. The hand caught Robert in the chest. 'If you come to scouts, you're dead.' Then Raymond followed his father and brother down the slope, past the lemon grove.

Robert looked towards the gate. A car, lurching up the drive. In it, Papa, and Dr Gabilier.

With a look of distaste, the doctor rubbed his hands in the water that dribbled from the kitchen tap. 'Nasty wound, tough little rascal.'

'What are his chances?' asked Papa.

The doctor wiped his hands on the kitchen towel. 'Hard to say. The wound's a mess, got some muck on it, some kind of ointment, he's got a high fever, oh, and possibly a chest infection.'

Papa stood up quickly. 'Hadn't we better get him to hospital?'

The doctor shook his head. 'Out of the question. I'm afraid you're stuck with him, for the time being.' He made for the door. 'You'll have my bill in a fortnight. I know it used to be monthly, but how things are, who knows where we'll all be in a month's time?'

The door clapped behind him.

Lise stood up. Dizzy. Shivering. Edged towards the door.

Papa cleared his throat. 'Lise, there are some things I'd like to clear up with you.'

She looked at him. He blinked. 'Are you all right?'

She shook her head, wanted to run to him, hug him. *Why did I lie?*

The small parlour door opened. Maman. To her husband, quietly. 'I think you should know, he's woken up.'

The boy was staring at the ceiling.

Head, foggy, what's that smell? People?

Moustached man leaning over him. Must be the dad. Slow talker, means well, sad-looking. What's he saying?

'– one or two questions if you can?'

Jaq nodded. *Agree, agree, always agree.*

'Very well.' Georges Durelle drew up a chair and sat beside the couch.

Jaq narrowed his eyes. *Who else?* Woman, by the window, reddish-blonde hair, lit up in the lamp. Mother? Ma? The kind of eyes that see right through you. Careful. The man's asked another question.

'– name?'

Jaq shuddered.

The hardest thing to know is, how much to tell them. To get the best result. And these people, they seem so good. Easy meat – but, you can never be too careful –

The father bloke leans closer. 'I asked your name.'

'Jaq.' *Why not?* 'Jaq Crouzier.'

'And you are from?'

'Charleville.'

'Has the fighting reached there?'

The boy coughed. 'Ask my ma.'

He turned his head aside, and spat carefully into the waiting handkerchief. *Good. Some blood in the spit.*

The woman, the mother, spoke for the first time. Voice like thick cream. 'Is your mother safe?'

He shut his eyes.

The father bloke coughs. 'Is your mother well?'

'His mother's dead.'

The girl. Lise. In the corner. With the sad face. What's she told them?

Maman, Papa, they're looking at Lise. She hangs her head. Then the mother looks back at Jaq.

'Is that right?'

He nods. 'Bombed out.'

Lise calls out again. 'That's why he's come down here, looking for help, and what do they do? Shoot him.'

Papa looked at Lise. 'You seem to know a lot.'

Jaq tried to lift his head. 'We talked. She helped. Don't blame her.'

The father leans closer. The room seems darker. 'Is this when you were in the shepherd's hut?'

His head fell back. As it fell, he caught the girl's eye. With a big effort, he nods. 'That's right, the hut.'

The mother glides closer, holding out her hand.

What's your game? He flinches away.

'Your temperature.'

Awkward, he lets her cool hand settle on his brow. 'What happened to your mother?' she asks. 'Do you mind talking about her?'

He shrugged.

'Were you with her? When she died?'

Jaq stares into space. He speaks in a monotone, as though repeating a lesson he's learnt by heart.

'It was early. There was no warning. I was in the kitchen, trying to light the stove. Heard aircraft. Ma put a pan on, with two eggs, one each, to boil. Old man Gaspard, the concierge, he came stamping up the stairs.

"Parachutes, parachutes!"

I ran down to look. Sure enough, over the river, they were coming down like snow. Huge planes, droning, banking.

"Are they ours?" Old Man Gaspard says.

Then the bombs. First one hit the grocers up the road. I ran. There were fires all round. Noise. Smoke. The ground was shaking. The planes came in so low, swooping just over the roof tops, firing. *Rat-a-tat.* When they'd gone, I walked back home. Rubble, smoke, water spraying out of pipes. Then the next street, everything normal, shops, they were still open, people were in the shops, shopping. When I got home –', he looks up at her. With his fingers he fiddles with the fringe on the blanket, 'the whole front of the house was blown out. All the rooms, open, like a doll's house. I could see our kitchen, the sink hanging out by its pipes and the washing rail, and the cooker. The pan was still on the cooker.'

He looked away.

'And your mother, did you see her?'

'Yes. They didn't want me to, but the bodies were stretched out on the pavement, round the back, out of the way, they had them covered with bedding, and I sneaked up and I pulled the sheet back, and I had a look. I said goodbye.'

Yvette squeezed his hand. It was ice cold.

Georges cleared his throat. 'You were lucky not to be in the house yourself.'

Jaq looked away again, and pulled his hand free.

Silence.

'I'm sorry about your mother,' the woman says.

Jaq's shoulders squirm. Croaks out. 'Me too.' His eyes are filming, closing.

The woman stands up. Her hand's gone, leaving his brow open, exposed.

'What's the state of the fighting?' asks the man.

Yvette puts her hand on his arm. 'Not now, Georges. He's talked enough.'

Chapter Eleven

Pigache heaved up the tool bag, and hurled it to one side. The hut shook. Raymond and Bernard clattered among the sieves and rakes.

'What a load of old rubbish the old Itie keeps in here,' grumbled Pigache.

'Funny,' grunted Raymond, 'there's no sign of blood.'

The door creaked open. The Pigaches stopped and turned. In the doorway stood Giuseppe.

'Aha,' said Pigache, 'maybe you'll be able to help us find what we're after.'

Lise lit the two lamps, one at each end of the big parlour. She shivered. She could hear the faint sound of the radio from her father's study. News. The droning, scary official voice.

The house felt strange. Everyone tiptoeing. Lottie on her knees in the corner, drawing.

Robert slouched in. Threw himself on the big couch, as though trying to make a big noise.

Silence.

Robert picked at the threads on the antimacassar.

The door opened. Papa. He hesitated, as though surprised to find his children in the room.

'Robert, isn't it time you went to scouts?'

'I'm not going.'

'Yes you are. And Lise, I want a word with you.'

As she followed her father into his study, she glanced out. Three figures crossing the yard. Giuseppe, leading Pigache and Bernard.

Giuseppe points, past the barn, towards the water pipe. 'There, that's where I saw it.'

Pigache nods. 'Come on then, show us.'

Robert hesitated. The scout hall smelt of damp and paint. From the big room the high excited voices of boys playing. Robert braced himself and pushed the swing door open.

Boys, dressed in brown uniforms, chasing, scuffling, laughing. Feet clattering on the hollow floor.

For a moment the noise carried on, a chaos of shouting and screaming and laughter.

Then it stopped.

The hut was quiet.

'Look who it isn't,' giggled André.

Pretending to strangle André, was Raymond.

Robert tried to smile. 'Hello.'

'Hello yourself.'

Raymond let go of André, and straightened up, swung his fist, hard, towards Robert's stomach. Robert collapsed, flinching away. Raymond stopped the punch short.

All the boys giggled.

Raymond grinned.

Robert straightened himself.

'I'm sorry about this afternoon,' he said.

'Sorry doesn't pay no ground rent,' Raymond said.

'He can't help it,' giggled André.

Raymond turned on André, frowning. 'What do you mean?'

'He can't help sticking up for a stinking thief, cos he's a stinking thief himself!'

The boys roar. Some uneasy, some glancing at each other. But they all join in.

Raymond is grinning again.

'That's right,' he says. 'You're just as bad as he is, and your stinking sisters. And as for your mother, my father says what she needs is a good seeing to –'

Robert's stomach twisted, but he kept trying to grin. And nod. Felt sick. Scared.

Raymond advanced on Robert, so his face was very close. 'If anyone said that about my mother,' he hissed, 'I'd knock him down. But you, you're such a filthy little dishcloth, you just laugh about it.'

'Cos it's true,' spittled André.

'His mother's a whore!' someone else calls out.

Robert stops smiling. He's twisted up inside, frozen to the spot, caught in the foul closeness of Raymond's big face: there's a light-green crust under Raymond's flat fat nose, green sleep in his eye corners, and round his lips the remains of something brown – gravy?

'Make him beg!' someone shouts out.

Raymond presses even closer. So close, his small eyes are like two crawly insects.

'Will you beg?' he hisses.

Robert tries to speak: 'It's not my fault.'

'Kneel!' someone shouts.

And then others take it up. Until they're all shouting, chanting: 'Kneel, kneel, kneel, kneel.'

Robert slips down on to his knees. His face is level with Raymond's waist, where his loose shirt hangs open. His trousers are grubby and creased.

'You are my slave,' grins Raymond. And he flaps his hands lightly at Robert's head, once on each ear. Not hard. Just enough to bring the blood stinging to the surface. Then Raymond turns and grins at the others. But, he's run out of ideas.

André says: 'Make him promise.'

'Swear an oath,' someone shouts.

'Oath, oath, oath,' the others join in.

Raymond puts his big hands around Robert's neck. 'Will

you?' The big fingers tighten and squeeze. Not pretend. Not fun.

Robert nods, and nods, and nods. Gasps, 'I'll swear, anything.'

Raymond gives one more good hard squeeze, so for a moment Robert's windpipe is crushed, and the air can't get down. Then Raymond pushes him back, and throws him. Robert hits the floor, and squirms away, to the side.

Raymond turns to the others. 'What shall I make him swear?'

'I've got an idea,' says André slyly, 'a sort of challenge.'

The door opens, and Monsieur Tettelin comes in. Glances at Robert on the floor. Ignores him.

'Who's on flag duty tonight?' he asks.

Lise sits in her room, where she's been sent, by her father. 'Until supper time.' In her hands she toys with the Marchesa. *Stupid doll.*

Papa, so solemn, so righteous. 'Please go to your room and think about what you've done, and whether what you've done is right or wrong. There will be no lock on your door, because we trust you to do as we ask.'

Not knowing is worse than knowing. Lise gets up quickly, paces. Sits again. Creeping dread, all up her chest, so she can't breathe properly. *Have they found the bag?* Every sound, every silence, is it them, did Giuseppe show them?

Dark now.

Well, even if they find the bag – so what? He swore on his mother's grave. Nothing to fear.

She tried to write a letter to Hélène, in her head.

'*Hélène, you'll never guess, we've caught a thief, I hid him –*'

But every time she started, the words stung her too much.

Her door clacks open.

Robert. His hand over his face.

'What's the matter?' Lise asked.

He sat down on her bed. Took his hand away. His eye was black, and under it bulged a red lump the size of an egg.

Lise knelt down beside him. 'Raymond?'

He flinched away. Stared at the wall. 'You help thieves, but you won't help your brother. I know that.'

'Course I'll help you, if I can. I've always told you, keep away from Raymond, he's just a big fool and a bully –'

Robert touched his swollen cheek, winced. 'He had a bag, didn't he?'

'Who?'

He turned quickly to her. His eyes were wild, scared. 'Who do you think? Your friend, the thief.'

Lise shook her head. 'Have they found it?'

Robert stood up. 'No, but if I find it, I'll be all right.'

'Why?'

'If we get the bag, it sorts it out for all of us. Because, if there's nothing in it, nothing stolen or illegal or anything, then your friend's in the clear. So it's good for him too. Don't you see that?'

He looks to her again.

Lise stares back at him.

He takes her by the shoulders. 'Do you know? You do, don't you? Where is it?'

Lise pulled herself free. 'No I don't know.'

Robert got up. 'Well, I'm going to find it.'

'So,' asked Monsieur Gossan, 'what did you find?'

Pigache swigged at his wine. 'Nothing but a rag in the stream. That blasted fool Giuseppe showed it as proud as his mother's jewels.'

'More fool you,' crowed Monsieur Montbleu, 'for letting yourself get bested by a petticoat!'

The bar rocked with laughter.

Pigache drained his glass, and flung it so it shattered in the fireplace. The chuckles died away. 'Skirt or no skirt, I don't give a skunk's muff for that little basket's chances.' He nodded, and waved a hand. His eyes were red.

'You seem a little troubled,' suggested Montbleu.

'I'm not troubled!' Pigache slapped his hand on the table. 'Strangers!' he cursed. 'They never bring any good.'

'Maybe he's a refugee, an innocent refugee,' said Gossan, with a sneer.

'Refugee from what?' demanded Montbleu.

'From the north.' Gossan eyed his tumbler of rouge, then swallowed it. 'That's what I hear tell. Hundreds of them. Driven from their homes by the Germans, so they say.'

'Driven!' Pigache spat into the hearth, then stood up, picking up his pouch and carbine. 'Driven! I'll give you driven. The Germans are pussycats. Our army's knocking seven bells of beg your pardon out of them. It's only the chancers, the rogues, the thieves who come whinging and begging down here. They want to stay up there and fight, like my boy, Marcel!'

Gossan nodded. 'I hope he's all right?'

Pigache thrust out his chest. 'I should say so, ready and eager to do his duty.'

He strode to the door, and slammed it behind him.

The other men looked at each other, with raised eyebrows.

'Shame,' said Gossan.

'The whole business really seems to have got to him,' added Gérard.

'It's no joke,' said Montbleu.

They all nod and murmur knowingly.

Gossan slaps the newspaper with his hand. 'A stranger's one thing, and a thief's another, but when you read this it makes you think. The Germans are sending paratroopers disguised as nuns.'

'And priests,' added Montbleu.

'For all we know, this thief, he's a spy, a fifth columnist,' reasoned Gossan. 'It's our duty to do something.'

'And what about that Durelle fellow?' said Monsieur Gérard, with a cunning look. 'Who knows what side he's on?'

'He won't fight for France, that's for certain,' nodded Gossan.

'He doesn't mind fighting against us!'

They nod again, and drain their tumblers.

'One way or another,' announced Gérard, 'I say the whole lot of them need teaching a lesson.'

'That's right,' said Monsieur Tettelin from the shadows of the doorway. 'What we need to do is make an example, *pour encourager les autres*.'

Chapter Twelve

Lise took the heavy torch off the hat stand.

The big front door groaned as she pulled it open. The insect door slapped on the frame. Dark. No moon. The air was cold. There was a hiss of something in the undergrowth.

Out of sight of the house, Lise flipped the switch, and a thick band of creamy yellow light splashed over the path.

Something scuttled up the barn wall, and clattered on to the tin roof of the lean-to. A gekko, sickly greenish in the torchlight.

Lise leapt down the path, scudding and skidding. The grass whipped wet on her ankles. Her heart slapped and jumped inside her. The frogs croaked.

The sluice ladder clattered under her feet.

She shone the torch round the sluice. Just as they had left it, when Giuseppe carried Jaq up the ladder. Look at it. Without him here, pathetic, empty, pointless. The plate, the flask, the stupid picnic basket. *Like playing house*. Screwed up on the floor, the map torn from the geography book. '*Northern Italy and Switzerland.*' Might as well be Mars. Quickly she packed the things into the basket.

A fox screeched.

One thing left to do. Robert's words echo in her head: '*the bag, that'll sort it out for all of us*.'

She climbs up on the plinth. Reaches up behind the green pump. The mulch and muck, it's been scraped away. Instead, a hollow. A hole where her heart should be.

The bag has gone.

Robert licked his lips. Felt in his pocket. Glanced round, over each shoulder. Then pushed into the small parlour. In his hand was his scout knife. Carefully, he pulled it open. Cautious, he stepped to the camp bed. The boy's urchin head, thrown to one side, the mouth open, the eyes shut.

Robert slowly extended his arm, pointing with the knife towards the boy's face. Robert's mouth twitched. He began to whisper.

'You don't fool me. You're not half as sick as you make out. I wish you'd fallen down the mountain. Don't think you'll get it easy. Just because my parents are so good. Don't think you'll get away with it. I know about you, I know your sort. I know you're a thief. Everyone hates you. Why don't you die, and leave us alone?'

The boy shuddered.

Robert flinched, then stretched the knife closer. His hand was shaking.

'It's my task,' he whispered, 'to slit your nose.' He laughed, a soundless laugh, jaw slack, head nodding. 'Raymond Pigache, that's the deal, I swore an oath, if I want to be his friend, I've got to slit your nose. Nothing personal. No hard feelings. It's just what they do to thieves round here.'

The boy's eyes opened, dull, filmed over. Robert shrank back. With an effort, the boy raised his head a few centimetres from the pillow. His lips moved.

'Cut me, then.'

The ladder banged against the concrete wall as Lise climbed.

In her hand, the basket. In the basket, the plate and mug. She's breathing quickly.

The thought of the bag's dragging round her stomach.

Who found it?

Lise pauses, sniffing at the air.

What is it?

She clicks the torch off.

Trees melt and merge in the gloom, shadows loom.

She listens. Croaking frogs, yes, insects chirping. But, something else?

Coming from up the hill, near the house? A low, long hissing?

Lise peers up the hill.

Lights. Three, four, five. Not electric torches, but real

flames, on sticks. The smoke flies in wisps and gushes. Dark figures, carrying the torches. Something strange about the figures, their silhouettes, about the shape of their heads: pointed at the top, and smooth-sided like rockets. Then she realises. They are wearing hoods.

Lise runs, back up the path, bent double, trying not to make a noise, not to bang the basket, not to breathe.

The flaming torches are in the yard. Figures, bustling, hissing, swaying the lights. Darting this way and that.

Lise edges her way along the wall of the small barn.

Inside the small barn, Malcio howls, then sobs.

Now she is closer, Lise can see the hoods better. Home-made, out of old curtains, or shirts. Loose, clumsy stitching. She edges towards the house. The basket scrapes against the wood of the barn.

The nearest hood jerks his head round, peering straight towards her.

Lise shudders, flat like an insect against the rough wood. Have they seen her? What are they doing? What do they want?

The hood moves on, nearer to the house. They're gathering together now. They start chanting, not loud, but in a kind of whisper.

'Stranger, thief, stranger, thief!'

The front door swings open.

Lise's throat lumps up.

It's Papa, wrapping his long white dressing gown round himself. His hair is tousled, his white feet are bare. He calls out, calm, matter of fact: 'Hello, there. Can I help you at all?'

'France for the French!' someone shouts.

'Thief lover!'

Then they stop, as if they don't know what to do next.

One of the hoods reaches up to the washing line hanging across the yard. On it, two shirts, a pair of drawers, and Lise's belt, washed clean of blood. The hood yanks at the line. The shirts dance like hung men.

'Come on!' he shouts. Three, four, five pairs of hands reach up and yank at the line. The line wrenches free of the post. The washing tangles in the dust.

The ringleader takes a step forward. In his hand he has a lump of rock. 'Let's teach these swine a lesson!'

Crash!

The hissing erupts into a long drawn 'Ye-sss!'

That's a window gone.

There's a scurry as other hoods stoop and pick up rocks, stones, bricks.

'We want the thief!' shouts the ringleader.

'Let's go in and take the bastard!' shouts someone else.

'I'm sorry,' says Georges Durelle, 'but I can't let you do that.'

'We'll see about that,' blusters one hood.

'It's none of your blasted business,' shouts another.

Yvette appears beside Georges on the porch. Their hands touch.

Another rock clatters on to the porch next to them. The

hoods gather and hesitate, as though needing just one more kick to push them over the edge into action.

Georges Durelle straightens his shoulders, tenses.

The door clacks open behind him.

The hoods hush.

Silhouetted, a small figure, in a loose white gown.

Lottie. Her face very white.

In both hands she holds a revolver.

Georges Durelle stares at the revolver. The hoods stare at him.

'He won't dare!' someone shouts.

'He's a peace lover.'

'Come on.'

They surge forward.

Crack!

The hoods stop in their tracks. Stare about, startled. Lise clicks on the flashlight, and yellow light glares on her father, and the hoods, and Yvette – in her two hands she holds the revolver. From its muzzle smoke trickles.

On the farm wall, smeared in red paint, are the words 'Death to traitors!'

In that moment, the hoods have gone.

Chapter Thirteen

'Who were they?' Lise whispered. The shadows from the candles dance on the kitchen walls. Cold air blowing in through the broken window.

Robert shook his head, shivered, a handkerchief clamped to his hand.

'I know them well enough,' grumbled Grande Tante, clanging the kettle on to the hob. 'They call themselves the Brotherhood of France-for-the-French, or some such nonsense. Farmers, shopkeepers, they think they're safeguarding the holy purity of France by playing kiddy games in fancy dress.'

'Why should they care so much about one boy?' asked Lise.

Grande Tante poured the hot water into the mugs. 'Because they're scared of what they don't know. The sooner the police take him away, the better.'

'What about the revolver?' Robert asked. 'Where did that come from?'

Grande Tante stirred the *chocolat*. 'Though he doesn't

boast about it, your father was a soldier in the last war. He fought for three years.'

Maman came in from the small parlour, carrying the scout knife. 'Is this yours?'

Robert looked at the knife. 'Yes. I must have left it on the table.'

Robert took the knife, and his mug, and hurried off up the stairs.

'Is the thief dead yet?' Grande Tante asked.

'Georges is seeing to him.'

Grande Tante tutted. 'Our Georges, I don't know what's got into him. He does the nursing, and you fight the battles.'

Yvette looked at Lise. 'Why were you outside?'

'I heard noises.'

'Why didn't you tell me?' Her voice was sharp.

Lise swallowed. 'I just thought it was Malcio.'

Maman shook her head. 'I'm sorry.' She tried to smile, reached out and touched Lise's cheek. Her long fingers were cold. 'It's not your fault.'

Robert was waiting for Lise on the landing. Furtive, hunched, eyes bright. He drew her into his room. It smelt of rabbits.

Lise glanced quickly around. 'Did you find the bag?'

Robert shook his head. 'I looked everywhere. Did anyone say anything about his nose?'

Lise shook her head. 'Why?'

'That was my task.'

'What do you mean?'

'To be Raymond's friend, I had to cut the thief's nose.'

Lise pulled away. 'How could you?'

'I didn't. I couldn't. He said, go on. But I couldn't, cos I'm weak and useless.'

'That's not weak, you were right not to do it.'

'Right?' he looked up at her. 'Right? I'd rather be friends with Ray and them, than right.'

He held out his hand, and pulled away the handkerchief. There's a thin cut along the back of his wrist, in the shape of a cross. Pinpricks of blood well up at the ends. 'He cut me.'

Lise couldn't sleep. The sheets were sticky, twisted. Her chest churned, her head flashed with the crack of the revolver, the cut on Robert's wrist, Maman's sharp voice, worried face, the shapes of the hoods. *What if they come back?*

She slipped out of bed.

'Where are you going?' hissed Lottie.

'Nowhere.'

Lise tweaked the curtain aside and looked down. There on the porch, on a kitchen chair, sat Papa. His head was lolling, then he jerked upright. On his lap was the revolver.

Lise slipped back into bed.

A shape padded across the floor, and squeezed in beside her. Lottie. Leaving just a centimetre gap between her small hot body and Lise's. Lise put her arm round her sister, and drew her closer. 'You were really brave tonight.'

Lottie sighed, snuffled like a hedgehog.

The black mist was rising up Lise's neck, but then she jerked awake again. Some fact, some thought. A sensation. Uncomfortable, not right. What?

The bag – and the hole where it ought to be.

Chapter Fourteen

'Of course I take it all seriously.' Officer Picard was a big, distinguished-looking man, with a square head like a block of stone, a tiny neat moustache, and cropped, silver-grey hair. He was circling the yard, making notes in a tiny notebook with a tiny pencil.

'Persons in hoods?'

Papa nodded.

Picard stooped by the water butt. 'What's this?'

Lise swallowed, hard. With some distaste, Picard was examining the basket she'd dropped the night before.

'Plates, a flask – looks like they were having a picnic.'

Lise hurried over and picked up the basket. 'It's mine,' she said. 'We were playing at houses.'

As she put the basket under her arm, she caught a glimpse of Giuseppe approaching up the track. Seeing Picard, he ducked down out of the way.

Picard creaked himself upright, and moved on.

Stopped and dabbed with his toe in the dust.

'Damage to washing line?'

'And they smashed a window.'

Picard peered at the plywood board nailed up over the broken window. 'You actually saw one of these hooded persons throw the stone?'

Georges Durelle licked his lips. 'No. Not exactly. They picked up stones. I heard the crash.'

'Did you *see* them pick up stones?'

'It was dark, I saw them stoop. There was no one else here.'

'Can you identify who threw the stone?'

'No.'

'Can you identify any of them?'

'Obviously not,' said Georges, 'that's the point of the hoods.'

Grande Tante bustled out of the kitchen. 'I've lived in these parts as long as you have, François Albert Picard, and we both know very well who these clowns are. Give me your pencil and I'll make a list of names for you, shall I? Starting perhaps with a certain baker who is also your brother-in-law?'

Picard raised a hand. 'Without evidence, I can do nothing.'

'And you want a quiet life!' added Grande Tante.

Picard tapped his notebook. 'Everything has been noted and will receive due process.' He turned to Georges Durelle, nodding towards the holster on his belt. 'Including the discharge of a firearm.'

Georges drew the revolver out of the holster, and offered it to Picard.

'Where did you get it from?'

'In the last war, I was a soldier.'

Picard peered closer at the weapon. 'This is an officer's revolver.'

'Yes, I was an officer.'

Picard handed the revolver back. 'Still gives you no right to go round firing it.'

'He didn't fire it,' interrupted Grande Tante. 'It was his missus, God bless her.'

Picard nodded. 'Where is Madame Durelle?'

'Gone to market.'

'To buy food for the family,' added Grande Tante. 'Is that a crime these days?'

'No,' mused Picard, 'but given the circumstances it might not be wise.'

Lottie clutched her mother's hand, tight. As they walked along the row of stalls, a hiss of whispers followed them.

'Ignore them,' Maman said loudly.

Every stall was surrounded by a clamour of women, shouting, and leaning and waving their purses.

'Why's it so busy?' Lottie asked.

'I think everyone's worried that food will be in short supply, so they're in a panic, and buying much more than they need.'

'Hadn't we better buy something?'

'That's what we came for,' replied Yvette, and headed for the nearest stall.

Lise sat very straight in the tall chair. Picard sat on the corner of Papa's desk, swinging a booted leg. He always makes Lise feel guilty. Just the way he looks at you. Now, he was staring straight at her. A disapproving look. 'There's a couple of things I'd like to straighten out.'

Lise nods, squirms on the hard chair.

'Where did you find the thief?'

Lise bit her lip. 'I found him in the shepherd's hut.'

'Did he have a bag with him?'

What to say? 'I didn't see one.'

'No valuables?'

She shook her head.

'No crucifix, you know, a cross with Jesus on it?'

She shook her head.

'Not the kind of thing you want to lie about,' mused Picard. 'A holy thing, might bring bad luck and curses if you lied about it.'

Lise forced the words out: 'I've seen no crucifix.'

No lie.

'And the chicken?'

'He left that, when the dogs chased him –' She bit her mouth shut.

Picard leaned closer. 'But you did see him, with the

chicken, earlier on?'

'A chicken, yes.'

'What colour?'

'Brown – with a red crop.'

Picard made a careful note in his book. 'And how did you get him from the hut to here?'

'I didn't. Giuseppe helped me.'

Picard turned to Georges. 'Is he about?'

'I haven't seen him today.'

Lise kept her mouth clamped shut.

Picard nodded. 'No. That old rogue'll keep well out of the way when there's police about.'

He turned quickly back to Lise. 'And I believe the thief, he threatened you, with a knife?'

Lise shook her head. 'No, certainly not, he didn't.'

Picard stood up. 'Now, I'd better see the thief himself.'

'How much longer?' Lottie pressed herself into Maman's legs.

'Until we're served.' She opened her purse, counted, then shut it again. Looked over the stall, the empty boxes, the shrivelled leaves and blackened potatoes.

The stallholder briskly swung a bag across the stall, to the customer next to Yvette. Yvette opened her mouth. The stallholder swung away, as though Yvette didn't exist.

A customer whispered something to her friend.

Yvette stared her in the eye. 'Have you got anything you want to say to me?'

The woman shook her head. 'There's no need. Actions speak louder than words.'

Chapter Fifteen

Lise picked her way carefully down the steps by the water pipe. Pretending to be casual. Pretending to kick at the grass.

'Are you looking for something?'

Giuseppe crouched by the side of the path. Sweating. Uneasy. Shifty. Working on the wheel of his handcart.

Lise swallowed. 'Maybe.'

'Something someone lost?'

Why mess about? 'The bag. The boy's bag. It's disappeared.'

Giuseppe nodded. 'Last night. I see your brother searching.' He reached into his hand cart. 'I think best if he don't find.'

Pulled out the canvas bag. Offered it to her, nervous. 'Don't tell. Don't say it's me. No police, OK?'

Lise took the bag. The canvas was tacky on her fingers.

'Hello, my friend.'

Jaq half opened his eyes. Who is this guy? Block-headed, bright eyes, tight uniform.

'My name's Picard, I'm acting commander of the police station in this area.'

The bed sagged under the officer's weight.

Creak of uniform, whiff of boots.

'I'd like to ask you one or two questions.'

Jaq nodded. Just the policeman, and the father bloke, standing by the window. The copper speaks.

'Your name is?'

'Jaq –' (cough) '– Crouzier.'

'From Charleville?'

He nodded.

'Age?'

'Thirteen.'

The policeman holds out his big paw. 'Your papers, please?'

Jaq shook his head, as if to clear it.

Picard shifted impatiently. 'Come. Your identity papers, your ration card, your residence permit.'

Jaq felt at his shirt breast with both hands, then shook his head. 'Lost.'

Picard stood up.

Jaq lifted his head off the pillow. 'The bombs, my house, my ma, we had to run, everything –' Then he coughed, and a froth of phlegm and blood bubbled on his lips. Georges Durelle went quickly to him. Picard snapped his notebook shut, watched Georges Durelle manoeuvre the boy on to his side, wipe at his mouth.

'Old Pigache, he shot him, a flesh wound.'

Picard stood back, frowning with distaste. 'Pity he didn't shoot straighter.'

Lise slid through the front door, stood in the hall. The bag was heavy in her hands. Heard her father's voice, then that of Picard, muffled through the small parlour door. *Maybe best to take the bag upstairs?*

As she put her foot on the bottom stair, the small parlour door opened.

'Aha,' said Picard, 'it looks like we have some evidence at last.'

Picard placed the bag carefully on the table. Stood back, like a conjuror. Glanced at Jaq.

'Is this your bag?'

His head lolled on the bed. *Don't say a word.*

Picard reached forward, and opened up the flap. Turned to Georges. 'If you'd be so kind?'

Georges reached into the bag. As he lifted each item out, Picard made a careful note in his notebook.

Jaq stared at the wall. *Stupid kid, bringing it. They've got you now.*

'Candlestick, silver? Napkin ring. Silver too.' He glanced again to Jaq. 'You like your silverware, don't you?'

Georges reached into the bag again. By the door, Lise held her breath.

'Flat iron. Clock.'

'Is that the lot?' demanded Picard.

'Only bits and pieces.'

Georges took the bag and upturned it. Lise eyed the mess quickly.

Georges shrugged. 'No crucifix, officer.'

Picard frowned. 'Young man, where did you get these things? Did you steal them?'

Jaq shook his head. 'My ma's things, her last things, after the bomb, I kept them –'

Georges Durelle held up some scraps of card. 'I think these might be the remains of his identity papers.'

'Let me have a look.'

Georges Durelle took the pieces and handed them one by one to Picard.

'Part of a residence permit, stamped for Charleville –'

'Out of date,' remarked Picard.

Georges pointed. 'But it does have his name and part of an address.'

'What else?'

'Part of an identity card.'

Georges handed it over.

Picard sniffed, and shook his head. 'The photo is missing, and part of the first page, and something's been scratched out under "Other comments".'

'The distinguishing features are there, though.'

Picard peered closer at the card, and then at Jaq, comparing.

'Chin, pointed. Mmmm. Nose, thin, hair, dark, face, pinched.'

'That seems to tally,' said Georges.

'Especially the pinched face,' said Picard.

Georges handed over the last piece of card. 'I think this is part of a food card.'

Picard took one look, and tossed the card aside. 'No name. He could have stolen it from anyone.' He turned to Jaq. 'These papers are hardly in good order.'

'What do you expect? I was bombed out in the clothes I stand up in, and I've been sleeping rough for a month.'

His head lolled sideways, and he snuffled his nose into the crisp linen of the pillow. Eyes half shut. *No crucifix*. That's taken the wind out of their sails. Smart kid. *Dud papers*. So what? The blockhead policeman, he'll never check. Will he? *That's all we need*. Maybe, maybe not. *Live to fight another day*.

Picard clipped the notebook shut.

Good. All done. Jaq let his head loll further over the pillow. Another cough. The dad bloke feels at his pulse.

Wait for it.

Picard turned to Lise. 'If you could leave us.'

She crept out of the door.

Georges let go of Jaq's wrist. 'Are you going to take him into custody?'

Picard shook his head. 'Can't. Not my jurisdiction.'

'But he's in danger here, and my family –'

Picard pulled on his cap. 'Proper procedures must be followed.'

'So what happens next?'

Picard reached into his large pocket. 'All a bit messy. Trespass, proven. Threatening behaviour, no witness. Theft of crucifix, no evidence, theft of a fowl –', he nodded towards the door, 'One witness – your daughter. There'll be charges. But, he's a minor. So he says. So I can't lock him up. And then, unsatisfactory documents – he'll have to be processed. That's a job for the Civil Administration. I'll let them know, and they'll take it from there.' From his back pocket he pulled a set of handcuffs. 'In the meantime, we'd better make use of these.'

Lise jumped back from the door where she'd been listening. Inside the room, there was a snarling, something clattered, Picard swore.

The door opened. 'What more proof do you need?' Picard sucked at his hand. 'Biting and scratching like an animal.'

He turned to Lise. 'Thank you very much for your information, young lady, you've been most helpful. Oh, and you may need to give evidence, about the chicken, as a witness.'

Jaq tugged at the wrist cuff. *Keep calm.* The bed creaked. Should have gone, should have left, last night, the night before, whatever. *Trapped.*

Don't give up now. *Make a plan, make a plan.* Got to be smart.

Glances towards the door. Who's that?

The door opens slightly. In the doorway, staring at him with big solemn eyes, is a small girl.

'Do me a favour?' he croaked.

Lottie stood, motionless.

'Go and fetch your ma, will you?'

Lise struggled up the dusty lane. The basket pulled on her arm. Inside the basket the chicken clucked. Lise's heart clucked and jumped along with the bird.

One lie piling on to the others. She's shutting herself off from Maman, Papa. They can't help her. *Only you can help yourself. And what you need is to make everything all right.*

Make everything all right. The words echoed in her head, in rhythm with her feet on the dusty track.

She hesitated at the farmyard gate. The lopsided postbox, with 'Pigac . . .' scratched on the wood, in childish letters. In the yard, everything dirty and broken.

Did she dare?

Her heart surged inside her.

Yes, she dared.

She flicked the frayed rope loop off the gate post, and edged through the small gap. The gate was heavy. A bucket lay in the dust, rusty, left where it had fallen. Dog mess everywhere.

The two fat shaggy dogs lumbered up to her, sniffing. The chicken grumbled. Old Pigache was sitting on the step of the porch, cleaning his shotgun. He stumbled to his feet. 'Clear off! Keep away!'

Lise forced herself to say what she'd been practising in her head. 'I've brought you something.'

Pigache peered past her, nervous, looking for someone else. 'We don't want it, we don't want nothing of yours.'

A spark of anger flared in Lise. 'Then why did you come in hoods and smash our windows?'

Pigache squinted, waved a hand impatiently. 'Now wait a minute, I heard about the little visitation, but I'll swear you this. It wasn't me or mine. That's not how a Pigache does his business, not in masks in the middle of the night. If I've got business, I come to your front door, and I knock on the knocker.'

Behind Pigache, a curtain twitched.

Lise spoke quickly. 'They found the boy's bag, he didn't have your crucifix, so I brought a chicken to make up for the one he took –'

Lise put the basket down. Did the curtain twitch again?

Pigache glanced round, edgy. 'That's a Christian thought, and let no man say a Pigache spurned a Christian thought.' He stooped quickly and grasped the handle of the basket. 'Not that it makes your thief any less of a thief.' He breathed deeply. 'Now, I'll thank you kindly, you've done what you wanted, I'll say good day.'

Lise held her ground. 'Are you going to press charges?'

'That's my business, now clear off.'

A face appeared at the window. Bernard? No. Lise stared.

'What are you staring at?' Pigache barked.

The face had gone.

Lise looked back to Pigache. 'I thought I saw someone.'

'No you didn't.'

Then she remembered. 'I did – it was your son, Marcel – is he home from the war?'

'No.' Agitated, Pigache stepped up and down on the porch, wiping at his forehead with the gun cloth. 'You're seeing things.'

Lise's mind was racing. 'Monsieur Pigache, if you press charges, then Officer Picard, he'll have to come round here again.'

'So?'

'He might see what I've seen.'

'You little devil!' Pigache grasped both her shoulders with his two hands. He leaned his face so close she could feel the spit as he spoke. His red eyes burned. 'Now, missy, listen, and listen well. You've seen nothing, and you'll tell no one, you forget what you think you saw, and I'll forget about the chicken, and the crucifix and everything else, God help us. Do you understand?'

She nodded. He let go of her. 'Now go. And remember what you promised.'

* * *

'It's a disgrace!' Yvette Durelle pursued her husband into his study. 'Whatever the boy's done, there's no reason to chain him up.'

Georges sat down. Every word seemed to cut him. Nodding, shaking his head, fiddling with his papers. 'But you didn't see him, like a wild animal –'

'Is it any surprise, if you treat him like one?'

'And he is a criminal –'

'A suspect,' corrected Yvette. 'Not formally charged, let alone convicted.'

'But Picard is a representative of the law, we have to do what the law tells us –'

Yvette shook her head. 'If I didn't know you better, I'd say you were scared. That you want to get rid of him, because he's a nuisance –'

'A nuisance? He's more than that, when a gang of maniacs comes after him smashing the place up.'

'All the more reason to look out for him.'

'The law will look after him.'

'How?'

Georges lowered his eyes. 'I expect he'll be taken to the internment camp at Agde.'

Yvette pressed on: 'You told me how awful it was, the conditions –'

She reached out and put her hand over his. 'Do you think I'm enjoying this? Do you think I enjoyed it this morning at the market when Madame this and Madame that whisper behind my back and snigger and point fingers and Madame Galaup serves everyone else their vegetables first, so all I get are the pigs' leavings?'

'Do you think I wasn't terrified last night? Do you think I want to bring danger on my children? But think of it this way.' She took a breath. 'What if something happened to you, and to me –'

'Why should it?'

'You know it could.' She snapped her fingers. 'Like that. At any moment. And if it did happen, and Robert, and Lise, and, God help us, Lottie, were on their own. With no one to look out for them. Don't you hope, don't you pray some good person, some stranger, would try and help them?'

Georges Durelle squirmed in his chair. 'Our children aren't thieves.'

Yvette pressed his hand. 'Because the world hasn't made them thieves, yet.'

The words hung in the air.

'What should we do?' His voice came out as a whisper.

His wife stared him in the eyes. 'You know what we have to do.'

Georges slid open his desk drawer.

'I swear I won't cause no trouble.'

Jaq rubbed his wrist, shook his head. *So far so good.* Dad bloke, hovering at the end of the bed. The ma woman stands over him. *Something about her. Makes you look away.*

'There's no need to swear,' she says.

'I only bit the man cos I can't stand being shut in, chained up.'

'Whatever you've done, we won't allow this.'

And she tosses the cuffs to the dad bloke, and he catches them, all guilty.

She's still talking in that calm, strong voice. Not a voice you can ignore, or interrupt. 'We want to talk straight to you. You're in trouble, and we want to help you.' She paused, and fixed him with her dreamy eyes. 'For us to help you, you need to help us. We need to know the truth about you and what you've done.'

Jaq's squirming in his head, like a worm caught on a hook. 'You want to know what I've done? What I've done wrong? Shall I tell you?' His head's tilted back. His face pale, fierce, serious.

The ma woman sits down. So close. *Smell her, like perfume.* He's blinking, there's pattering in his chest. *Keep calm.*

Yvette reaches out and touches his hand. He jerks it away. 'Truth is, I've done some things I shouldn't. In these last few weeks.'

'What things?' The ma woman's eyes are like searchlights, probing. Have to look away.

'I never had no money. So food, I begged. And –', cough, looks at her with a pained expression, '– and I stole things.'

'What things?'

'Food, and a shirt off a washing line, this shirt –' Jaq

plucked at the remains of his shirt. '– and rides on trains. I didn't have the money for tickets.'

Are there tears in his eyes?

The ma woman leans closer. 'You must have been very hungry.'

He nods. 'Round Dijon, I went two days and only a mouldy cabbage I found in a ditch. I know stealing's wrong, and I'd never steal if I had food for my mouth, but if you're starving, what else can you do?'

The ma woman stands up, looms over him. 'I understand.' And before he can stop her, with a gentle swoop, she's kissed him, once, gently, on the forehead. There's the tang of her sweet smell, and the softness of the lips, and suddenly, he's crying. Crying for real?

Yvette picks up the scraps of identity cards from the table. 'Your name is really Jaq Crouzier?'

He nods.

'And your address?'

'Seven Rue de Joinville, Charleville.'

Yvette Durelle made a note in her pocket book.

The father's got his wrist, taking the pulse. 'It's only fair to say, the decision about your immediate future doesn't lie with us.'

Jaq lets his head slump sideways on to the pillow. 'I don't care,' he says, 'I only want a chance.'

The ma woman's looming over the bed again, the card scraps in her long fingers. 'Will you trust me with these?'

Careful.

'They ain't worth much. What do you want them for?'

'I hope my husband will take them to a friend of ours –'

'A forger?'

'No, he's an official, with the mayor's office.'

Georges frowned. 'You mean Pierre Bernadou?'

Yvette nodded, offered him the card scraps.

Georges turned away. 'I'm sure he'd rather speak to you.'

Chapter Sixteen

Lise half-skipped, half-ran back along the track. *Done it, done it, done it!* Bubbling over.

She stopped.

Blocking the yard was an old bread van, with a big sticker on the side, scrawled with the letters 'C G', and a flag on a bent coathanger mounted on the mudguard. Lounging in the driver's seat was Henri, Marie Trevette's older brother.

'Hi, Louse,' he called.

'What are you doing here?'

He leaned out of the cab, thrusting his shoulder at her. He wore an armband, sewn in red with the letters C G. 'Careful how you talk to me. I've just enrolled in the Civil Guard, and we've come to get your little crim.'

Monsieur Luffau was short, sallow, bespectacled. His black suit covered a pot belly. He carried a clipboard.

Georges led him through the kitchen. 'The thing is, my

wife's gone into town to talk to the civil authorities.'

Luffau smiles and huffs. 'A wasted journey, I'm afraid. Under current conditions, I am the civil authority.'

Georges opened the door into the small parlour.

Jaq lifted his head off the pillow. 'Is this the papers bloke?'

Georges sighed. 'In a manner of speaking.'

Luffau marched to the bedside. 'I'm in charge of identity verification in this district.'

Jaq narrowed his eyes.

Luffau checked his clipboard. 'According to the police report, your papers are not in order. May I see them?'

Georges coughed. 'My wife has the boy's papers.'

Luffau turned slowly to Georges. 'That is highly irregular.'

Jaq tried to sit up. 'They took them off me, I couldn't stop them. They said they were going to get things sorted out.'

'That's true,' nodded Georges. 'We didn't expect you to come so quickly.'

Luffau brushed a speck of dust from his sleeve. 'Oh, we work pretty fast, don't you worry, not like the old civil service.' He made an entry on his clipboard. 'Young man, you'd better get yourself ready for a little trip.'

'Where to?'

'The internment camp at Agde. It's by the seaside.'

Georges raised his hand apologetically. 'It'll only be temporary, won't it?'

'Only while checks are made.' Luffau smiled. 'As soon as your papers are sorted out, you'll be free as a bird.'

Jaq shifted on the bed. *Got to think fast.* 'I understand. It's just a bit hard to move.'

'Don't worry about that,' said Luffau.

Jaq swung his leg out of the bed. The bandage had come loose, so the wound was revealed. Luffau recoiled.

'Feel a bit sick –' Jaq faltered, and then a shaking takes the scrawny body, and a jerking, and his back arches, and then his head throws forward and out of his mouth gushes a stream of vomit, spattering on to the floorboards at Luffau's feet.

Georges Durelle has Jaq under the arms, trying to support him, but the boy sags sideways, and falls. Out of his mouth jerk words, whispered loud. 'Sorry, let me die, trouble enough.'

Luffau edged backwards. 'You don't fool me. It's the camp for you, you mark my words.'

Georges laid Jaq's head down. 'I'm not sure that's a good idea.'

'It's none of your business. We'll take him if we have to drag him.'

Georges followed Luffau into the kitchen. 'At least let me clean him up.'

'Of course.' Luffau put his head out of the window. 'Henri – quick.'

Henri propelled himself off the bonnet of the van and ran in. Lise followed him. 'What's the matter?'

Georges had a white enamel bowl under the sputtering

tap. 'Nothing to worry about.' He led the way back to the small parlour. 'Just a temporary –'

They stared through the open door at the empty room.

Luffau hurried out into the yard. He looked round at the trees, the slopes, the steps, the paths. He bent, and felt at a brown smear on the concrete.

'I think we've picked up the trail,' he said. He pointed up towards a rusty cow trough.

'Aha,' he said, 'I think I see something.'

Out of his pocket he pulled a large revolver. Fumbled with the safety catch.

'Is that necessary?' asked Georges.

'This counts as resisting arrest.' And he stumbled on up the path, with the gun raised.

Something moving, in the grass. Luffau paused, aimed.

'No,' shouted Lise, 'that's my sister.'

Luffau lowered his arm.

Lottie stood up, and scrambled down the slope. Her cheeks were red, as though she'd been crying. Georges picked her up.

'We're looking for Jaq, the boy, have you seen him?'

Lottie shook her head.

Luffau reached out and touched at her arm. 'Cut yourself?' She shook her head again. Luffau peered back up at the trough. 'Henri,' he shouted, 'see if there's any more *children* playing up the hill there.'

Henri approached the trough cautiously. He looked around, bending over, feeling in the grass. 'Nothing I can see –'

And then with a gasp and a grunt and a flurry of grass and arms he disappeared. Luffau and Georges hurried up the hill. Stopped.

Lying in the grass, was Jaq. One arm round Henri's neck, the other hand over his mouth. Jaq's eyes were milky. 'One step closer, and I'll kill him.'

Luffau clicked the safety catch on his revolver.

Lise shouted. 'There's a car coming.'

Nosing into the yard was a bright red sports car, its soft top thrown back. Driving it was an elegant young man with floppy hair and a smart coat. In the passenger seat sat Yvette.

'So you see, the boy's papers are in order.' Pierre casually tossed the identity card on to the big table. It slid along the polished wood. Luffau reached down and picked it up. 'I've not seen one like this before.'

Pierre leaned back in the deep armchair, crossed his legs casually. 'Oh, they're pretty common under current conditions. It's called a Temporary Residence Permit, it's used when people unavoidably get displaced. You can't be expected to know, being new to your post.' He turned to Georges, who stood stiffly by the window. 'What a wonderful day, have you found a buyer for your lemons yet?'

Georges shook his head.

Luffau tutted. 'But what's this stamp, and this one?'

'Let me see.' Pierre held out his hand, like a schoolteacher with a slow pupil.

Luffau marched over. He liked the sound his boots made on the wooden floor.

Pierre took the card, and casually pointed. 'This is the regional imprint, this is the town stamp, this is the mayor's permit –'

Luffau put the card back down on the table. 'Very well, very well. But there are other matters. The lout, he's a danger, a menace.'

Pierre laughed. 'He seemed quite a pussycat once Madame Durelle came on the scene.'

'You didn't see him in action.' Luffau turned to Georges. 'You saw him. I'm frankly surprised you leave your wife alone in there with him.'

'My wife has a mind of her own, Monsieur Luffau.'

Pierre raised his glass. 'I'll drink to that.'

Luffau shook his head. 'I still think something should be done.'

Pierre waved a hand. 'Fair enough old chap, take him away if you think that's the right thing. I'd have thought he's a police matter now, but I suppose there's not much chance you'll get pulled up for wrongful arrest or whatever.' He yawned. 'Frankly I couldn't care less.'

'Very well.' Luffau clapped his hat back on his head, and tried a smart salute. 'I'll double check the paperwork back at the office.'

Ignoring him, Pierre sipped his wine, and turned to Georges. 'Georges, old chap, what's wrong with you? This bordeaux is half decent.'

Luffau grumbled all the way to the van. 'Most irregular, most irregular.'

Henri, rubbing his neck, opened the passenger door for him.

'Monsieur Luffau!' exclaimed Grande Tante, waddling into the yard with the egg basket, 'not wearing your hood today, then?'

Luffau sat to his full height, sniffed. 'Madame, I'm here in my official capacity.'

Grande Tante sniffed back. 'What do we want with a wine clerk?'

'Maybe more than you bargained for,' retorted Luffau, and clapped the van door shut.

'He was a horrible little man,' Lottie said, as the old van rattled and groaned away down the track.

'It's his new-found rank,' said Pierre. 'I think it's gone to his head.'

'He has an important job to do,' said Georges Durelle.

'But why is such a horrible little man so important?' demanded Lottie.

Pierre Bernadou tousled Lottie's hair. 'Because all the good men have gone to fight the Germans, and only poor wretches like him are left.'

'But you haven't gone to fight. Or Papa.'

'Enough questions,' frowned Pierre.

Jaq lay on the bed with his shoulders propped. Yvette sat by the window, resting her elbows on the table. For some moments she looked at him, her hands clasped at her chin. He squirmed, and looked away. 'Go on then, say it.'

'Say what?'

'Have a go at me for trying to get away from the identity bloke.'

'I understand what you did.'

No you don't. Leave me alone.

She tapped her finger on the table. 'What are your plans now?'

What? Plans?

'No one's ever asked.'

'When your leg heals . . . You have new identity papers.'

'All I've done is try and get away from the fighting.'

Remember, it never pays to tell the truth.

'I was thinking we could find you somewhere to stay.'

'Like where?'

'There's a place, a very good place, quite near here. Up in the mountains. They take all sorts of people. Children. Who've lost their parents –'

'I'm not a kid.'

'Maybe not in experience, but in age –'

'I can't stand being cooped up, told what to do, institution stuff, dormitory things –'

He stopped.

'Have you lived like that?' Yvette asked.

'A bit.'

Why tell her?

She leant forward. 'Not all places are the same. This place I'm talking about, they're very liberal, very free and easy, like a family –'

Let her talk. Agree with her. His eyes dull over. Yvette stopped speaking. Just looked at him. *Leave me alone!*

'Very well,' she said, with a kind of smile in her voice, 'you don't want to go to the orphan school, what do you want to do?'

That's my business. 'I'm all right as I am.'

'But you haven't got any money, have you?'

He shook his head.

'You can't keep on running away, living rough.'

'It's been all right so far.'

'How long's it going to be before you steal something else, and they catch you, and then you'll be cooped up all right.'

He turned his head. Met her eyes. It's like some kind of warm cloud rising up his chest, an impulse, he can't stop himself.

'Fine. I'll stay here then.'

A frown passes over her face. *She wasn't expecting that.* Lay it on thick.

'I could work. There's loads of stuff needs doing here.

Look at the walls. They need painting. Your old man, God bless him, he's not exactly strong on bricolage, is he? I can do a bit of carpentry, labouring, you name it –'

The words flooded out. And it sounded so sincere. Like he actually believed it.

Yvette got up and walked to the window.

He stopped. Hardly breathing now.

She fingers the cracked plaster round the window frame. 'I hadn't thought of it.' Turns to look at him. 'For one thing we can't afford to pay you.'

'Who needs paying? I owe you too much already.'

She looks out the window. 'And it's only fair to say we've hardly got enough to feed ourselves, we're borrowing money, because Georges can't sell the lemons –'

She stopped. Jaq swallowed. A feeling like a boulder in his chest is swelling up. You're going soft. He looks down at his hands. The words come out much harsher than he means.

'You're right, it's a stupid idea. You don't want scum like me messing up your nice family set-up. You should have let Luffau take me away. Or the hoods. They know what to do with scum like me.'

'Yvette's certainly taking her time in there,' said Pierre, recrossing his legs on the chaise.

'She doesn't do things by halves,' Georges replied, examining the new identity card. 'Is this genuine?'

'Well,' laughed Pierre, 'you know what it's like with red tape. I just took an ordinary blank identity card, and I stamped it with every stamp I could find in the town hall. The old saying goes, if you can't convince an official, the next best thing is to confuse him!'

Lise looked up from the book she was pretending to read. 'So if he tries to travel, with those papers –?'

Pierre glanced at her, as though surprised to discover she was in the room. Shrugged. 'Who knows? If they fool one idiot, why not another?'

'I hope,' Georges said, 'you haven't done anything improper, or illegal.'

Pierre spread his arms. 'How can *I* do anything illegal? As secretary to the mayor's office, everything I do is entirely legitimate.'

And he laughed again.

Georges nodded. 'But isn't that strictly speaking committing some kind of –'

He waved a hand. Pierre eagerly finished the sentence for him. 'Crime, indiscretion, misconduct, outrage – yes, of course.'

The door opened, and Yvette came in. Pierre turned with a lingering look towards her. 'But when it comes to my friendship for you –' he nodded quickly to Georges, and then lower and slower to Yvette, 'and your family, you can be assured I will move mountains.'

'There are still other things to think about,'

'Such as,' laughed Pierre, 'how to offload that hooligan as soon as possible before he knifes someone good and proper.'

Yvette sat down at the piano. 'That's not what's going to happen.'

Both men looked at her. 'What do you mean, Yvette?'

'For the time being, Monsieur Crouzier's staying here.'

'That's madness,' said Georges.

'Who knows?' mused Pierre, raising his glass to Yvette, 'under a fine and beautiful influence, who knows what beast may not be charmed?'

Georges ignored him. Leaned towards his wife. 'You must remember, the decision isn't up to us, even with these so-called papers.' He slapped the card down on the table. 'There's also the matter of the stolen chicken.'

'I'm sorry,' said Pierre with a little bow of the head, 'but I have no influence when it comes to domestic fowl.'

Yvette tapped a finger on the arm of her chair. 'Surely we can sort that out. What's one measly chicken? What if we give Monsieur Pigache a chicken to make up for the one that's missing?'

Georges shook his head, paced to the window. 'I don't think that will satisfy him, or the law.'

Lise raised her head from her book. 'I think it will,' she said shyly, heart racing. 'I already took a chicken to Monsieur Pigache, and he seemed entirely satisfied.'

Pierre raised his glass to Lise. 'You may not have your mother's looks, but you certainly have her spirit.'

Georges Durelle stood up. 'Lise, I'd like to have a word with you in my study.'

Chapter Seventeen

Lise sat. The air fragile, artificial. Papa. Ever so calm and careful. As usual.

'You never think, do you?' Papa, pacing. Hands behind his back. In the parlour, Pierre laughs his high, carefree laugh. Georges Durelle glances quickly at the door. 'It's all very well,' he goes on, 'having high ideals and warm feelings, but just to act on impulse, it can be disastrous.'

Another laugh from the parlour. Georges keeps talking. 'You must remember, first, this boy is a criminal, we know nothing for certain of his background and, whatever happens, he won't be here forever.'

'Yes? So?' Lise's throat is tight, but she manages to keep her voice level. Her father looks to the floor. 'I'm trying to say that if you get too fond of him –'

He breaks off.

Lise's face is burning. 'What makes you think I'm fond of him?'

'You sheltered him, you took the bird, you took that risk –'

'What makes you think I did it for him?'

'Well, I thought – your mother and I thought, maybe you – liked him.'

'*Him?* He's caused nothing but trouble. I took that chicken to Monsieur Pigache so the hood men wouldn't come here again. That's why I did it.'

Papa nodded, sat down. Looked up at Lise across the desk. Her heart surged. From the parlour, another laugh, louder. Papa frowned, glanced at his watch, turned on the radio. 'In that case, you won't mind if you keep your distance from the young man from now on?'

'Are these the best you could get?' grumbled Grande Tante, picking at the blackened potatoes.

'Lucky to get any at all,' said Lottie.

'They were all buying like there was no tomorrow.'

'Maybe there won't be,' said Robert.

'Where's the salt?' demanded Lottie.

'Please!' added Grande Tante.

Maman ladled stew into a bowl. Robert watched. 'Is that for him?'

Maman nodded.

'Don't give him all the best bits.'

Lottie stabbed with her fork. 'There aren't any best bits.'

Robert took the bowl. 'I don't know why I have to wait on him.'

Grande Tante winked at Lise. 'Don't you wish it was you?'

Lise didn't look up. 'Where's Papa?' she asked.

Lottie made a face. 'In his study.'

'Listening to the radio,' sneered Robert.

'What's the matter with him?' demanded Grande Tante.

'One of his moods,' mouthed Lottie.

'Lise, you'd better go and call him,' said Yvette.

'And fetch the salt on your way,' added Grande Tante.

Jaq watched Robert edge across the room, and put the bowl down on the cabinet next to the bed. Jaq's hand snaked out and grasped Robert's wrist. 'What's up?'

Robert tried to pull his arm free.

Jaq held on tight. 'There's nothing to be scared of,' he said. 'There's an old saying: a grudge never sold at market.' He pulled Robert closer. 'So let's forget the nose, and you splitting on me.' He twisted Robert's hand round so the scab of the knife cut showed. 'See, in a way, we're like blood brothers. So if you do the right thing by me from now on, you'll stay healthy. Understand?'

Robert nodded.

Jaq lifted his head closer, hissed: 'And if you cross me, you'll be cut, and you'll be cursed.'

Jaq let go of his wrist. Picked up the bowl, spooned at the stew, made a face. Robert edged to the door.

Jaq glanced up. Casual. 'Where's your sister?'

'Which one?'

Jaq couldn't say the name. 'The big one.'

Robert gestured with his head. 'In there. She's not allowed anywhere near you.'

Lise pushed through the study door. The radio voice droned on. Papa looked up from his desk. Unshaven. He was wearing his vest, no shirt. Switched the radio off. 'What is it?'

His voice was dull, and his eyes.

'Dinner's ready, we're eating.'

He sat, his face set. Staring at the radio.

Lise shifted, awkward. 'Maman asked me to fetch you.'

He stood up, resting his knuckles on the desk, as though he might fall over.

'What is it?' Lise asked, half-reaching to steady him.

He turned and looked at her. 'Nothing, nothing at all, nothing to worry you.'

Robert, Lise, Lottie. They sat in a line in the big parlour on the settee. Maman paced in front of them. As she talked, she twisted her wedding ring. 'I wanted to explain to you exactly what's going on with our guest, Jaq. You know we always try and explain everything to you, discuss decisions with you.'

She paused.

Robert stared back at her. Lottie stared back at her. Lise stared down at the floor.

'You don't know what he's like,' said Robert, glancing at the door as though Jaq might be listening.

Maman nodded, paced brisker. 'I know he's from a different background to us, I know he can be a bit rough at times, but still, he's the guest, you're the hosts. It's up to you to make sure you all get on. Because, he's been through some terrible things, and it's our duty to help him and give him a chance. And I'm sure that if we do, he'll respond, and pay us back more than we give him.'

Lise looked up. 'I don't see how I can get on with him when Papa forbids me to go near him.'

'You're lucky,' said Robert.

Lottie was kneeling on the bed, shaking her finger at the Marchesa doll. 'And if you dare tell I'll cut you and slice you and make you into a pie.'

Lise sat down beside her. Startled, Lottie huddled the doll away. 'I didn't hurt her, I only borrowed –'

'I don't mind,' Lise said. 'What were you playing?'

'I promised not to tell.'

'Is it a game to do with Jaq?'

Lottie glanced round, then leaned closer. 'When the Luffau man was after him. Jaq said he'd kill me – if I showed where he was hiding.' She hugged the doll closer. 'So really, I saved him. Can I keep her?'

* * *

Gone midnight. Lise crept along the passageway. The small parlour door caught, and then gave as she pushed it. Pale moonlight washed the room. The bed was empty. Her heart skipped.

There was a scuffling, a bang, and there in the corner was Jaq, wrapped in a blanket, sliding his back against the wall.

She stood awkward in the centre of the room. The silence seemed to hum. Lise's head hummed too.

'Can't sleep,' he whispered, wriggling his shoulders against the cold plaster. 'Too quiet. What's up?'

'Lottie. My sister.'

'What about her?'

'Leave her alone.'

'What's she said?'

'The truth.'

Jaq shuddered. 'I only scared her a bit.'

'And my brother?'

Suddenly his hand was on her throat, pinning her back against the wall. 'You're all the same to me,' he hissed, 'means to an end, and I don't care how.'

His face so close, she met his angry, miserable eyes and held them. Her throat throbbed. 'You don't have to show off, not with us. Can't you get that through your stupid head?'

He stopped shaking her, let her go, and sank back on the couch. Lise edged nearer. 'We're not strong, we're not bullies. And my stupid mother's got this stupid idea she wants to help you. So that's what we're doing. So you don't have to threaten little girls and scare people.'

He was hunched, his knees clasped to his chest, chin pressed down. 'You don't understand. It's a different world.'

Lise swallowed. 'Like Grande Tante says, some people can't be helped.'

She turned away.

'Wait,' he said.

Lise stopped.

'It was smart,' he said, forcing the words out, 'what you did, with my stuff.'

'What stuff?'

'My stuff, in the bag –'

The floorboards creaked.

The door swung open. A candle swaying shadows. Papa. His face was pale, but now he had shaved, and he was dressed.

Lise hugged at her dressing gown. 'I'm sorry –'

'Please,' said Georges, 'go outside.'

He didn't look at her as she edged out of the room.

In the hall, she stopped. Something. A shape, grey in the gloom. Propped against the hall table. She tiptoed closer. A big sausage-shaped bag: grey and dusty, with all kinds of stains and tears and repairs. It was stuffed full, ready: Papa's army kitbag.

Georges Durelle didn't know whether to sit or stand. Uncomfortable. *In my own house. With a lout.*

The boy is hunching himself smaller in the corner.

'Don't blame your daughter. She just came to see how I was.'

Georges fingered the edge of the table. *Where to start? What to say?*

'In the morning, I'm going.'

'Where?'

'To try and join up with my old regiment.' He took a deep breath. 'The Germans have broken through all along the front. They're heading straight for Paris. I don't know how long I'll be gone. When, if, I'll be back. You're no fool. You know I never wanted you here. I'm no fool, either. I don't ask anything from you, I don't expect anything. Except, that you don't harm my family. That's all I ask.'

Jaq's chest was tight. 'Why should I harm them?'

'Because you can't help it. I know your sort. My wife, she's a very good woman –'

'The best,' said Jaq.

Georges swallowed. 'She always sees the best in everyone, but some people, whatever they try and do turns out bad.' Georges shook his head. 'Here.' He held out the identity card, fresh with stamps and seals. 'These are bad times. I wish you well.'

Jaq took the card, hard and smooth on his hand.

'Monsieur Durelle,' he said, 'I swear to you I won't do any harm to any of your family –'

'Please,' Georges interrupted. 'Please let's not descend to

oaths. They have a habit of getting broken.'

* * *

Lise waited in the hall. Listening to her father's voice. Muffled. Can't make out the words. The door opens. Out he comes. He stops, looks at her as though he doesn't recognise her. Lise, she can't speak. Waits, for him.

'Look after your sister,' he says, and walks past her, into his study.

Climbing back up the stairs, Lise feels dizzy. In her head, a madness. As though she is falling, and has no one to catch her.

Chapter Eighteen

Jaq woke with a start. *What's that?* He limped to the window. In the soft light of early dawn, the dad bloke's kneeling by the water pump, fiddling with the clasp, trying to get the handle fixed. Still half asleep, Jaq leaned on the window sill, and watched. Every time the dad got the handle lined up with the joint, the bolt fell out before he could hammer it through. But, he kept on trying, as the sun rose, and the roosters round the valley began to crow.

Why watch him? Sort of fascination. *Loser.*

A car coughed, then growled. Jaq, still leaning on the window sill, shook himself awake. The dad bloke's throwing this big bag into the trunk of the car. The ma's standing there with her hair down, watching. The dad bloke goes to her, hugs her, they're kissing.

Yvette stood back.

Georges opened the car door. 'I've fixed the pump,' he said.

'Say goodbye to the children?'

Georges shook his head. 'I can't.' He handed her something, yellow? Like a packet?

He opened the car door.

Lise raced out into the yard. The air was already warm. She stopped in front of her father. He ducks into the car. Slams the door.

Lise ran to the car door, pulled at it. 'Look at me, look at me!'

Her father looked away, and let out the clutch, and the car rolled away across the yard.

Jaq sat back down on the bed. Fingered the identity card. *Strange, strange, strange.* They've unlocked the door, and left him free. *Go, go now?* He limped to the door, listened, then knelt, and worked his fingers under the loose floorboard.

Lottie banged her two hands on the arms of her chair. 'I know why he's gone. He's gone cos he hates it here. Because he hates it with us. Ever since we moved to this place. All he does is moan and go sulky and lock himself away in his stupid study. He's not going to fight for France, he's going to get away from us.'

Maman was on her in a stride, picking her up by the shoulders, shaking her. 'Don't talk such nonsense.'

Lottie's eyes were wide.

'Yvette –' began Grande Tante.

Yvette put Lottie down. 'Remember this. Your father is the best man alive – the best. If you find a man a tenth as good and decent as he is, then think yourself lucky. He's straight, and he's honest.' She paused. 'Sometimes, in this world, a man can be too straight, too honest for his own good.'

The door opened, Jaq limped in. 'I wondered,' he said, 'if you had any jobs need doing?'

'Lock up your valuables,' called Grande Tante.

Yvette looked at Jaq. 'Yes,' she said, 'in a moment.' She reached in her apron pocket. Pulled out three yellow envelopes. Held them out to Robert, Lise and Lottie. 'Here. One for each of you. From your father.'

Lise took her letter out to her den to read. Wedged herself in the angle under the old work bench. Hidden. Hardly breathing. The sun shone in slabs through the slatted roof. The air was itchy hot.

'*My dear Lise,*

By the time you read this I'll be somewhere near the barracks at Orange. I'm sorry not to say goodbye, but I think if I tried to say goodbye to you and your brother and sister, I couldn't leave the Domaine, and to leave is my duty. I thought we'd done with all this. But now it's happening again, and we have to face facts. Every father's son, the same as the father. I swore I'd never fight again. But what else can you do, when a bully comes and threatens you, and your wife, and your children? In the end there's no choice for me. If everyone sat back and did nothing, the

Germans would be in our town by now, in our front room. I know these last few weeks I've been hell to live with. Maybe you'll all be happier without me. God grant I see you safe, and sound, in happier times.

I want you to know, that I trust you to be sensible, and to be brave, to help your mother, and to look after Lottie.

All my love, your father.'

Lise sat holding the letter, her mind blank. Gradually became aware of something groaning, straining along with her heart. *The pump!* Maybe Papa, he'd changed his mind, come back?

She scrambled up out of the lean-to. Stopped.

Jaq was wrestling the pump handle up, down, up. He was wearing a clean white shirt, and baggy brown trousers. A trickle of brown water spurted into the bucket. Seeing Lise, Jaq worked the handle faster, harder. 'I've been at it for half an hour,' he shouted.

Lise walked past him. 'Half an hour doesn't make a crook honest. Let me know when you've done it for half a lifetime.'

Maman appeared in the doorway. 'The pipe must be blocked up at the tank.'

Jaq let go of the pump, wiped his hands on his trousers. 'Where's that?'

'Up the slope.'

'I'll have a look.'

'What about your leg?'

'I'll manage.'

Yvette turned to Lise. 'Will you show him?'

Luffau walked briskly into the office.

Pierre Bernadou, lounging behind his desk, did not get up. 'Please have a seat.'

Luffau glanced around. The huge chairs, the high ceiling, the delicate plasterwork, the fine paintings. More like an art gallery than a serious place of work.

'No thank you,' he said, 'I prefer to stand.'

Pierre swung his long legs round, and landed his highly polished shoes on the edge of the desk. 'What can I do for you?'

Luffau struggled to restrain his gleeful irritation. 'It may interest you to know that I've made further enquiries about the proper procedures for dealing with persons with insufficient identity papers. It appears there is no such thing as a temporary residence permit – or if there is, it has no validity. Anyone issuing such a permit, in the knowledge of its lack of validity, will find themselves liable to investigation and prosecution for abuse of power and malpractice.'

His voice had risen to a kind of choked cry. He was pleased to see the Bernadou fellow pale, swing his legs off the desk, and sit up straighter.

Pierre tried a smile. 'Perhaps I should remind you that our system doesn't operate through threats and aggression.'

Luffau put both his fists on the desk and leaned closer.

His knuckles were white. 'No. Your system in the past has functioned through laziness, favouritism, nepotism, nods, winks, bribes, gifts and other degeneracies. If this war has done no other good, it's brought your corruption out into the open.'

Pierre's mouth had dropped open. He snapped it shut.

Luffau stood back again. 'You thought you'd made a monkey out of me with your rubber stamps and plausible explanations, but let me tell you this. I am no fool.'

'What's one refugee boy?' The words caught in Pierre's throat. Luffau ducked his head at him again, and Pierre shrank in his seat.

'You really think you're something, don't you, Bernadou? Just cos your family owns this and that, and you've got a college education, you think you rule the roost. Well you're mistaken. You see, old chap, you've had your day. You're past it. It's your sort who's let us down. We've got the power now. So in answer to your question, one refugee boy is nothing, nothing to me. What I want is you.'

And Luffau turned and walked briskly out of the office Pierre sat frozen, staring at his blotter. Then he picked up the telephone.

Jaq followed Lise up the slope, hop-stepping. He clung to grass, bushes, boulders, wincing as the bad leg dragged over the bristled dusty ground. 'Slow down a bit,' he puffed.

Lise stopped. Didn't look at him. Twisted at a button on

her blouse. His hair was so dark against the white of the borrowed shirt, his skin still so pale. He struggled up beside her. 'Are you talking to me?'

'I'm doing what I've been told.'

'By your ma?'

She nodded.

He grinned. 'Well. I bet she wants you to talk to me.'

Lise turned and carried on up the slope.

Jaq followed. 'Look,' he panted, 'have I threatened anyone since yesterday? Have I done any bad things? Can't you give me a chance?'

She stopped again. He was holding something out to her – a tiny flower, brown and yellow, like a bee.

'Oh, no,' she groaned, 'you idiot!'

Jaq looked down at the flower. 'It's for you. A peace offering.'

'It's a wild orchid. They're very rare.'

'That's why I chose it for you.'

'Now you've killed it.'

He laid the flower gently down on the ground.

She shook her head. 'Don't tell Maman, or Grande Tante. They'll send you off to Agde.'

She carried on up the slope, and he trailed along after her.

'Is this all your land?' he panted.

'Yes, as far as the stream down the bottom, and the road at the top.'

'Big.'

'Not big enough. We need another thirty acres to make it pay.'

'Who says?'

'Papa.'

'He's crazy. I'd make it pay.'

'What would you do, threaten people? Cut their hands?'

'I can work.'

'Oh yes, you can work, you'll make it pay, when my mother and father, they've worked all the hours God gives –'

'Yes, because I'm a winner, and them, beg pardon, they're losers.'

Lise hurried on, biting her lip.

Jaq followed, sniffed. 'Are we near the sea?'

Lise didn't answer. Scrambled up a steeper slope. Stopped. Jaq hauled himself up beside her. Put up his hand to shield his eyes. Licked his lips.

There, far below, was the sea, patched blue, and dark blue, and grey, and flecked everywhere with white as the wind whipped at it. Lise's thin dress clung round her legs.

'Where's the town?' Jaq asked.

'You can't see it from here. It's under the hill.'

'How far?'

'Three, four miles.'

Jaq pointed to the left. 'So that must be Italy.'

'If you're so clever why do you ask?'

He laughed. 'You don't hate me. Why pretend?'

He narrowed his eyes, and slowly took in the folds of

the mountains, the yellow pitted peaks rising out of the thick foliage.

'What's the border – a fence or something?'

'There's border posts on the roads, but once you get up into the mountains, it's just rocks.'

There was a rattling and a grumbling. Round the corner bumped a small truck, painted olive green. Two more trucks followed, then a small armoured car.

'Army,' said Lise.

Jaq stood up. 'Why are you whispering?' he whispered.

The first truck wobbled to a halt. The driver leaned out. His face was creased under the round helmet.

'What are you kids doing here?'

'My brother and me, we live here,' Lise said.

The driver spat. 'Well, you want to be careful.' He nodded back towards the border. 'Don't stray too close. There's thirty-thousand Ities with popguns lining up over there.'

Lottie clasped her mother's hand tight. They turned the corner of the winding road by the church.

Lottie pointed. 'Look at the beach.'

Yvette narrowed her eyes. The sand was covered with dark shapes.

'Are they penguins?' Lottie asked.

'No,' said Yvette, 'I think they're people.'

'But they're not sunbathing.'

And, as they got closer, they could see that all these

people were fully dressed – more than fully dressed, wearing coats over jackets over jumpers. Round them were bundles of belongings, bags, cases. A small child, sitting legs sprawled on the gravel of the beach, looked up with vacant eyes, and waved.

Madame Montbleu hurried past, clutching a large sausage. 'Whatever next?' she complained. 'Refugees, so-called, and I bet they want feeding.'

'What's a refugee?' Lottie asked.

'Someone trying to get away from the war.'

They walked on past the casino. Two men on ladders were pasting a poster over the doors. '*Closed till further notice.*'

There was a flurry of dust. A red car pulled up alongside them. Pierre Bernadou leaned out. His face was pale. 'Thank goodness I've found you,' he said. 'I've got some news.'

Lise stopped by a green metal tank set on a concrete base. 'This is where the water's supposed to collect. Then you pump it from the pump in the yard.'

Jaq squinted up the slope. 'Where does the water come from?'

Lise shivered, looked around. 'Up there somewhere. Trouble is, beyond the road, that's Monsieur Pigache's land.'

She wrestled the inspection cover open. Jaq leaned on the tank with both hands, peered in. 'Looks dry.'

Lise offered him a metal rod. 'Give the pipe a poke with this.'

Chapter Nineteen

Monsieur Montbleu threw down the newspaper. 'The question is, what's Italy going to do?'

'Nothing to bother us,' retorted Gossan. 'We're friends, and neighbours –'

'And they don't like fighting!' added Gérard.

'Haven't you seen the Blackshirts, parading up and down in Rome?'

'I mean, there's enough of the blighters living here anyway,' said Montbleu, uncomfortably.

'Half of Italy lives here.'

'Taking our jobs.'

'They could be plotting.'

'To take us over.'

'Make us all spaghetti eaters.'

The men murmured. Monsieur Tettelin tapped his finger on the newspaper. 'Something should be done.'

And they all nodded, nervously.

* * *

'Race you!'

Jaq was hop-stepping back down the terraces. 'Come on, I won't tell anyone, you can be horrible again when we get to the bottom.'

For a moment longer Lise hesitated, then the wind blew, and it was as though her heart soared up like a kite, and she plunged forward.

Jaq's face lit up, and he set off again. So quick, sliding and slipping. 'Can't catch me!'

She tried, jumping, cutting corners. He glanced back, and as he did his foot slipped, he stumbled, his leg gave way, he slithered with a thud down on his back on the path.

Lise knelt quickly by him, took his arm. Bony, thin. Their eyes met. His eyes were so dark, and serious. As though he knew sad things, things he never told. She ducked her head and kissed his cheek.

He sat up, pointed to a clearing among the olive trees. 'Who's that?'

Lise looked where he was pointing. 'Giuseppe.'

His white smock shirt hung open, vivid against the deep brown of his skin. He was trimming lopped branches with a bill hook, and tying them into bundles, whistling a tuneless whistle between his teeth.

'What's he up to?'

'Odd jobs, he hires himself out.'

'Giuseppe – is he Italian?'

'Yes and no.'

'How can he be yes-and-no Italian?'

'We're so close to the border, there's loads of yes-and-no Italians round here. Some of them live in Italy, but cross over every day to work. Then some of them settle here, but they're still Italians. And others, they've lived here so long, they have children, and the children grow up as French.'

'Does he cross over to Italy?'

'No, he lives just down the road –'

Giuseppe suddenly looked up, as though he'd heard something. Put a finger to his lips. Whistled. Glanced around, bent back to work.

Jaq leaned on a tree. 'Is he weird, or what?'

'No, he's just a bit of a loner. There's all kinds of stories about him, how he talks to ghosts and things. How he's got secret treasure stashed up somewhere cos he never spends any money. But he's always been fine with me. It was him who carried you into the house.'

Jaq glanced at her. 'And I suppose,' he said slowly, 'he brought my bag as well.'

'Yes, that's right, he did.'

'That explains it.'

Giuseppe looked up again, sniffed, then turned. Stared straight at them. Lise waved, awkward. Giuseppe threw down his hook and hunched his way out of the trees.

'Come,' gestured Giuseppe to Jaq. Giuseppe turned to Lise. 'You, go home.'

* * *

The door of the ramshackle hut creaked open. Jaq stepped in. The place was stuffed with tools, and chests, and cans, and bunches of herbs.

Jaq's quick eyes widened.

'My things,' said Giuseppe. He reached behind a box of hinges, drew out a tin flask, unscrewed the cap, and swigged. Held it out to Jaq. Jaq took the flask, threw his head back. The wine fired in his throat, made his head sing.

Giuseppe sat down on a canvas stool, gestured Jaq a log. Jaq sat. Giuseppe swigged again. His eyes were quick, nervous. 'You hate the policemen?'

Jaq nodded.

Giuseppe nodded. 'Me too. Bad times, I have with police back in Italy. Very bad times.' He coughed. 'You have bad times with Pigache?'

Jaq nodded again.

Giuseppe coughed again. 'Me, I have bad times with Pigache too. So –' He stood up, reached up to a high shelf, and pulled down something, something heavy, wrapped in a yellow duster. Clapped it down on the bench. 'It's yours. You take, or leave. Me, I never seen it.'

Robert ran panting along the track. *Had they seen him?* Behind him, someone hallooed. He darted in among the trees. *Quick.*

Just as Raymond and his gang came into sight, Robert

caught a branch, and hauled himself up into a tree.

The red car pulled up smoothly in the yard. Pierre yanked up the handbrake. 'So you see,' he said, 'no official order has come through yet, but I strongly advise you to prepare yourselves to leave the area at short notice.'

Yvette opened the door, she and Lottie climbed out. Pierre leaned from the window. 'I know how stubborn Georges can be. If he takes any persuading, let me know. I'll fill him in.'

Yvette brushed back her hair. 'Georges isn't here.'

'Where's he gone?'

'To Orange, to try and rejoin his old unit.'

Pierre shook his head. 'The fool, the stupid, stupid fool.' Cleared his throat. 'Now, where's the young man?'

Lise picked her way slowly along the path towards the house. *Jaq. Maybe he'll catch her up?*

Despite herself, a letter's writing itself in her head, to Hélène. *'The boy, it's very difficult. Maman thinks she knows him, but she doesn't. He's very rough and he was nasty to Lottie. But then he smiles and makes a joke and everything's so different, like the air's fizzy, and then his eyes. You look into his eyes, and there's such sad things there.'*

She stopped, lingered. Giuseppe, and Jaq. *Odd, how jealous she felt.*

The growl of an engine. Far below, on the road, a red

shape darted in and out of view among the trees. She stopped. Another sound? A rustling? She hurried on quicker than before. Turned the corner. Ahead, the kissing gate: leaning on it, André.

'Good afternoon,' he lisped. 'What's the hurry?'

'I smelt you, and I wanted some fresh air.'

'That's not very nice.'

She moved to push past him, but he blocked her way, and there was more rustling behind her. She looked round. Raymond, and flanking him half a dozen more of his cronies.

'Not very nice at all,' said Raymond. 'Not a polite thing for a nice girl to say.'

Lise tried to walk away, but two, three of the cronies had her by the arms, their faces close.

'Maybe she's not a nice girl.'

'Maybe she's like her ma.'

'Maybe she likes having visitors.'

Raymond pushed his big face closer to her. 'Do you like having visitors?'

Lise clenched her teeth.

'What about thief visitors?' said Raymond. 'You like them, don't you?'

'They're engaged to be married,' spittled André.

'Oh, you love your gyppo thief do you?'

'She was out with him,' André said, 'she went out with the thief this morning. I saw them up the hill.'

Lise's chest was hurting. 'I haven't any idea where he is,'

she managed to say.

'Oh,' said Raymond, with a big smile, reaching out his dirty hand to touch Lise's cheek, 'we don't want him. We want you.'

'We've decided,' André said, 'you need teaching a lesson.'

'Go on,' urged the cronies, shaking her arms so her head jerked forward, 'give her one.'

'It's all proper and legal,' Raymond said.

'We did a courtroom.'

'And you've been found guilty of making friends with the enemy.'

'So,' said André, 'you'll have to be punished.'

The cronies growled their approval, and the hands on her arms gripped tighter.

'Pun-ish, pun-ish,' chanted the cronies.

'Go on Ray, give her a seeing-to.'

'No,' said Raymond, pushing André forward. 'This is a strangle job for you.'

André glanced round at the cronies. 'I think I can oblige.'

He put his face close to Lise and whispered, so quiet only she could hear: 'I've always liked you.'

Then he touched her cheek.

Lise's mouth was dry, but she managed to suck up some saliva, and spat it. It landed on his chin.

André startled, felt the spit, then smiled again. Rubbed her spit into his face. 'I like that,' he said.

'Go on, go on, do her, do her,' the cronies urged.

André raised both hands, and moved them forward like a robot, until the palms were round Lise's neck, but not quite touching. Lise swallowed. The hands closed. André was grinning.

'Tighter, tighter, tighter,' urged the cronies.

André squeezed, so his palms bulged in her windpipe. Lise's eyes bulged too. André shook her slightly.

'That's the way,' growled Raymond.

'Tighter, tighter, tighter.'

André squeezed tighter, and shook her more.

A kind of squawk flew out of Lise's throat. Someone was pulling at the belt of her dress.

Robert jumped down from the tree. Stumbling, he wrenched André aside. Lise gasped in air. Robert had André by the shirt, but now the cronies had *him*. They were laughing and jeering.

'If it ain't Bob-face.'

'Haven't seen you around.'

'Thought you were dead.'

'He soon will be,' said Raymond.

André broke free, and knelt, puffing, rubbing his elbow.

'Now,' said Raymond, turning to Robert, 'what are we going to do with you?'

Robert's eyes were bright with fear and anger. 'I don't care,' he spat, 'do what you like you fat stupid freak. I've always hated you, and despised you, all of you, ever since we moved here.'

Raymond frowned. 'So that's how it stands. *Despise*, is it? That's a long word for a dishcloth like you.'

'Any word you like, you and your stupid games and oaths and courtrooms and dares. You're like seven-year-olds. My little sister's got more sense than you lot put together.'

André stumbled to his feet. 'I know what to do,' he said.

They all turned to him.

'Let's make *him* do it.'

'Yes, that's right, excellent.'

'And if he won't –'

André drew a finger across his throat with a slitting sound.

'Good call,' said Raymond. 'That's your choice, Bob-face.'

Two more boys held Robert's arms, and dragged him towards Lise like a lump of meat hanging between them.

'It's up to you,' said André, 'either you teach her a lesson, good and proper, or you get it.'

Raymond aimed a casual kick with his boot at a rock. The metal toecap thudded into the loose stone. Shattered shards splintered off with a puff of dust.

Robert was pale, blinking, twitching with fear. Lise met his eyes.

'Don't worry,' she murmured. 'I understand.'

The boys swung Robert back, then forward, back, then forwards. 'One! Two! Three!'

They catapulted him so he thudded into Lise, and they fell together in a heap.

'Again,' shouted Raymond.

'Look out!' called André.

But before Raymond had time to turn, in a flurry, a rush, Jaq was out of the bushes, a thick bare branch in his hands, and he'd swung, clubbed Raymond, twice, three times, on the back of the legs. With a howl of surprise, Raymond crumpled, sank to his knees. Jaq swung again, a wide swing with arms stretched. Too late Raymond got his hands up: the club smacked into his face, jarring his head back, sending him sprawling.

The others ran.

Stepping over Raymond, across him, Jaq swung again, and again, big blows, crashing into Raymond's ribs, the side of his head. Raymond wailed, hands over his head, trying to wriggle away.

Jaq was on him, his knee in the small of Raymond's back. Caught him by the hair and wrenched his head back. A tooth was missing, blood welled up. Raymond's dirty cheeks were streaked with tears. His throat stretched taut. In his free hand, Jaq had a knife.

'No!' shouted Lise.

Jaq looked up, his eyes dark, clear.

'No,' shouted Lise again. 'If you kill him, you'll never be free.'

Jaq hesitated, then pulled and twisted Raymond's head so he could see his face.

'If you ever,' Jaq hissed, 'if you ever try it on, any stupid thing, with any of us again, I'll kill you, understand?'

Raymond nodded, nodded, nodded, his big head jerking up and down. Jaq threw Raymond's face down so it smacked into the dirt, climbed off him, kicked him in the ribs. Winced with the pain of it. Raymond wriggled, snivelling like a baby.

'Get out of my sight!' Jaq shouted, aiming another kick.

Raymond got clumsily to his feet and lumbered off, clutching his mouth.

Robert picked himself up off the ground, backed away.

Jaq leaned against the kissing gate, breathing heavily. The borrowed shirt was smeared with blood.

'Are you hurt?' Lise managed to say.

He shook his head. 'Don't tell your ma.'

'You could have killed him,' Lise said.

'I should have.'

'That's stupid talk.'

Jaq closed his eyes. Spoke in a monotone. 'You ask your old man.'

'He's not like you.'

'If you don't finish them off, they come back. Like we should have finished the Germans off in the last war. Now they're coming back, and fatty Ray boy, he'll be back with his brothers and stuff.'

Jaq turned and limped down the track towards the house.

Chapter Twenty

'Where on earth have you been?' demanded Maman. She was kneeling on the floor. In front of her was a suitcase, half-packed.

'Trying to fix the water,' said Lise.

'It's back on,' said Lottie, sat on the floor, a tiny suitcase in front of her. She sipped from a tumbler. 'And it's disgusting.'

'Why are you packing?' Lise asked.

Maman stood up, handed her a holdall, Robert a valise.

'It's a precaution,' she said, 'in case we have to move out.'

'Why should we have to move?'

Yvette searched a drawer. 'If we're attacked.'

Grande Tante waddled in with the egg basket. 'And who's going to attack us? Seagulls? The Germans are five hundred miles away.'

Yvette flushed. 'According to Pierre Bernadou, the Italians are bringing troops and equipment up to the border. Special troops. Blackshirts.'

'Stuff and nonsense,' retorted Grande Tante. 'We may give ground to the blasted Germans, but we're not going to let the Ities push us around.'

'We saw our soldiers pulling back from the border today,' Lise said.

Yvette folded a blanket into the case. 'Apparently the main defensive line will be the other side of the valley.'

'So we're totally defenceless?' Grande Tante sounded less certain.

'And,' said Robert, 'if there's fighting, we'll be the first to be attacked?'

Yvette nodded. 'That's why it's best we get ready to move at short notice.'

Grande Tante picked up her knitting. 'Well, you won't catch me running away. I'd rather die in my bed.'

'Shut up, I don't like it!' Lottie put her hands over her ears. 'I want my papa.'

Grande Tante wrapped her arms tight round her. 'Yvette, think of the children when you talk, please.'

Maman glanced at Jaq, turned to Robert. 'Can you find a couple more old shirts and trousers for Jaq?' And to Jaq. 'I'll find you a case.' She went out into the hall.

Jaq made to follow.

Grande Tante took him by the arm, pointed at the smeared blood on his shirt. Whispered. 'Just to let you know, young man. You may fool some soft-hearted fools, but I know you, I know what you're like, and remember, I'm watching you like a hawk.'

She let his arm go, and he followed Yvette out into the hall. She was crouched under the stairs, wrestling with the mound of bags and baggage.

'When you've packed,' she was saying, 'I wonder if you could give Robert a hand scalding the milk churns? So we're ready to go – as ready as we can be.'

Jaq folded his arms over the blood smear on his shirt. 'Beg pardon, Mam – Madame, but why don't you go now?'

'Because the order hasn't been given yet.'

'If you wait for the order, it may be too late.'

Yvette licked her lips. 'I may be wrong, but I'm trying to stay calm and think things through. If we run away, who looks after Maya and Mizzi and the chickens? Where do we go? Grande Tante, how far can she walk? Who protects our things here? All my husband's work on the lemons will be wasted. And once we've gone, how long do we stay away? Monsieur Durelle and I talked all this through, and we agreed that we should stay as long as we can, and not to panic. If everyone starts running away, the roads'll be blocked, our troops won't be able to move, no one'll be able to get anywhere.'

'That's just my point.' Jaq tried to look her in the eye. 'That's why it's best to be one jump ahead.'

'That's not the way we are.' She straightened up, holding a battered old rucksack. Her face was pale. 'Anyway, I'm not sure how we're going to manage. I mean carry everything. There's a barrow in the garage. Maybe you could have a look at it?'

'Sure.'

He turned to go, she touched his arm. 'If you want to leave, please go. I can spare you a little money, some food, bread –' She hesitated. 'The only thing is, you won't be able to go till tomorrow.'

'Why not?'

'Pierre Bernadou, he needs to see you.'

'Why?'

'Some technicality. He said he'd come again tomorrow. The good news is, he's getting a proper check done, with the authorities in Charleville. The results should be in tomorrow, and then you really will be free.'

'That's good,' Jaq said, and took the rucksack, and limped away down the hall.

Lise breathed deeply, tried to calm herself. She felt numb. Going? Where? The little black hold-all was old, soft leather. It smelt of holidays. She put it open on the bed. Took this dress, that skirt, put them in, took them out, a towel, knickers, socks.

Outside, the clouds had broken, and the sun poured through.

She listened.

A cock crowed somewhere across the valley.

She tried the bag. It was already heavy. The house was so quiet. *What was Jaq doing?*

In her head, playing over and over, the thwack of the branch, Raymond's face, bloody, the tooth missing. She shuddered, and yet, somewhere in herself, anger flared. Raymond's stupid face, the feel of his fat fingers on her arms: somewhere, deep in herself, she was urging Jaq on, *hit him, hit him, hit him.*

She shivered.

And what about Papa? Is he fighting now?

The thought sent her head spinning.

The door opened. Lise jerked round. Lottie, head down, case in hand.

'Are you all right?' Lise could hardly say the words.

Lottie glared up. 'No thanks to you.'

In the garage-barn, Jaq squatted by the barrow. Old. Rotting wood. The front wheel was loose. He listened. Everything so quiet, so calm, so still – like madness. And a bigger madness, poised like a tiger. The war, ready to swarm over them.

Mad too, this other feeling, like an emptiness inside, a gnawing, a lack. Like you've failed at something. 'Go *if you want to*.' His flesh, he's squirming all over. 'I'm watching you.' Silly old bag. *What is it? You care what they think?* Jaq shook his head. Fool.

He kicked the barrow, stood up. Pulled open the drawer of the work bench. *Rubbish.* Like everything here, old and useless and worn out. Full of oily rags and frayed rope ends.

Not even worth stealing.

He squatted again, and tried to tighten the axle bolt.

It's like their strange stupidity is infecting you. They're losers, all of them. But it's as if you're starting to feel – what? His skin crawls. Shudders.

'*Good news – a proper check with the authorities!*' *Great.*

There's one more thing.

It's niggling away at the back of his head, so shaming he can't think it out loud, but it crowds up on him. It's the memory of him standing in the hall, talking to the ma woman, how it came out, without him thinking, how he nearly called her 'Maman', and only just managed to swallow it and turn it into 'Madame'.

He shook his head like a wet dog, yanked the spanner another half turn. The bolt bit, then gave. His knuckle slammed into the side of the barrow. *Thread gone*. The barn door creaked.

'What?'

Robert looked in. 'The old dear said you might want some help.'

Pigache hurried out of the house, dragging a heavy trunk. 'Raymond!' he shouted, 'give us a hand.'

Raymond slouched over, took a handle, and they swung the trunk up into the back of the mule cart. Pigache looked at his son. 'What happened to your teeth?'

'That thieving little stranger.'

Pigache shook his head. 'More fool you for meddling.'

Marcel Pigache peered out of the open door. 'What stranger's this, Ray?'

The cases are neatly stacked in the hall, smaller on bigger. In the centre is Grande Tante's massive trunk.

'I don't know how we can move that,' said Yvette.

They're sitting at the table, awkward. Papa's chair empty. Jaq, extra, squashed in next to Lottie. Head down, squirming in his seat, picking with his thumbnail at the varnish of the table leg.

Grande Tante spreads her arms. 'If your Georges hadn't gone off with the car, we'd be all right.'

Yvette turned to Jaq. 'Did you fix the barrow?'

'I tried.'

Robert sniffed. 'It won't take that trunk.'

Grande Tante shrugged. 'We'll hire a cart, why not?'

Yvette carried the pot over from the oven. 'It was mad in town. Everyone packing. I doubt if you'll find a wheelbarrow, let alone a cart.'

Lottie nodded. 'The roads were blocked with scarecrow people. We saw the police and the soldiers and everyone's whispering and buying potatoes.'

Grande Tante peered sideways at the pot. 'I don't know where we're going to go anyway. We can't go into town. What do we do with the cows?'

Yvette opened the pot. 'We have to take them with us, make our way across the valley.'

Lottie pouted. 'I don't want to go anywhere.'

Grande Tante pinched Lottie's cheek. 'We won't be going anywhere, you mark my words.'

Yvette delved into the pot with the ladle. Grande Tante wrinkled her nose. 'It smells of cat's pee. What is it?'

'It's salted fish; you have to soak it and boil it.'

'So long as we don't have to eat it,' Robert said.

'I bet it's really nice,' Lise said.

'Where's the salt?' demanded Robert.

Grande Tante made a face. 'You won't need salt with this.'

'How will we know when to leave?' Lottie asked.

'They'll send us a postcard, of course,' Grande Tante said.

They sat round the big table, picking at the watery fish. White with dark skinny bits, bones, and a deep salty tang that not even the garlic could hide.

Grande Tante chewed. 'I don't think you soaked it long enough.'

'There wasn't any water, was there?'

'Wasn't it soaking long enough in the sea?' Lottie asked.

Robert pushed his plate away. 'I'm not eating it,' he said. 'It's disgusting.'

'In hard times you eat what's put in front of you,' Grande Tante said. But after a few more picks and prods she gulped, and laid her fork neatly across her plate.

'I'm full,' she announced.

Only Jaq cleared his plate, sucking at the bones, licking his fingers. Lise watched, her neck burning. Robert sniggered, 'Manners!'

Jaq glanced up, Robert shut his mouth tight and looked away.

'That's a good lad,' said Grande Tante, shovelling her leftovers on to Jaq's plate, 'but don't think you've got round me.'

Yvette went into Georges' study, and turned on the radio. That droning voice again. Lise hovered at the door. 'Any news?'

Maman looked up. 'They never tell us anything. "The situation is serious without being desperate".'

'Where do you think Papa is now?'

Yvette shook her head. 'I wish I knew.'

The mood in the bar was turning uglier. Men swigged at their wine, and took it in turns to tell stories about foreigners taking advantage of French generosity.

One thick-set man with a heavy beard shook his head. 'We're fools unto ourselves.'

'It's got to stop.'

'Enough's enough.'

'The Germans, they wouldn't put up with it. They kick all the Jews and scum out of their country.'

The door opened. They all turned guiltily and stared at the squat, moustachioed man standing in the doorway:

Marcel Pigache. He looked round the bar.

'What are you doing back here?' demanded Monsieur Montbleu, uneasily.

Marcel walked slowly to the bar. 'The Germans,' he announced, 'are only five miles from Paris.'

The room erupted, a riot of shouting, clattering of tumblers. Excited men jabbed fingers in each others' chests.

'It's a disgrace!'

'Where's our army?'

A fist hammered on a table. The men quietened down. Marcel Pigache stood up. 'I'll tell you where our army is: fighting the wrong enemy. It's madness fighting the Germans. The only way forward for France is to join them. The real enemies are the Commies and Jews and the treacherous useless English.'

'And the outsiders,' called Montbleu, 'coming here, taking our jobs.'

'And the fifth column, dressing up as priests, and women,' added Monsieur Gossan.

Murmurs of agreement spread round the bar.

A single voice called out from the back: 'And you, Marcel Pigache, what are you doing here, when you should be at the front with the army, defending our country?'

Marcel Pigache shouted, 'Front? There is no front. The generals are fools, the politicians are rogues and milksops – I didn't run away. What was there to stay for? Our brave boys are surrendering in droves. We had no officers, no equipment, the Germans were all round us. You don't realise what it's like up there. Listen,' he pounded his fist on his chest, 'I have fought, I've seen the battle, and I didn't fight for strangers and dirty foreign swine to come and eat all my meat while I'm away, and beat up my family and steal stuff and get away scot free.'

Murmurs, agreement. 'No, that's right.'

'Chuck them out.'

'Get rid of the lot of them.'

'France for the French.'

Marcel Pigache hammered his fist on the table again. 'The question is, what are we going to do about it?'

Chapter Twenty-one

Lise sat at the piano in the big parlour, touching this key, that key, very gently, so the notes hardly sounded. Lottie crouched by the doll's house, murmuring under her breath.

Robert looked into the room. 'Stop that noise, will you? Either play it or leave it alone.'

Lise slammed the piano lid down.

Lottie banged the Marchesa doll on the floor. 'Don't, you scared me.'

Robert plumped himself down on one of the big, dusty armchairs.

Lottie asked, 'Where's Jaq?'

Robert sniffed. 'Reading this book Grande Tante gave him.'

In his room, Jaq sat chewing his fingers. His chin tucked on to his knees, the book on the floor beside him. Trying to shut out the feelings from the rest of the house. But, every creak and sigh and word from the family made him squirm and fret.

Every step on the stairs. He felt like a dog's corpse full of maggots. *Leave me alone, leave me alone.*

Rubs his hands, blistered from the screwdriver. The house creaks.

It's like hell here.

Now is the time to go.

A knock at the door.

He picked up the book.

Lise edged in.

He glanced up at her.

'Oh,' she said, 'Grande Tante's *Saint and Martyr* book.'

He nodded.

Lise sat on the bed. 'She must like you to give you that to read. What do you think of it?'

He squirmed his shoulders, shook his head. 'I can't make sense of it.'

Lise shivered. 'Those pictures, they always used to scare me.'

Jaq pointed with his finger. 'They're all the same story. Some guy or woman, they get in trouble, and what do they do?' He jumped up and threw the book on the bed. 'Do they run for it? No. Do they lie? No. Do they fight? No. They just sit there like fools and get it in the neck – killed on their knees.'

'Father Robideau says that saints are special people.'

Jaq laughed. 'Special? Sure – wrong in the head.'

'I suppose,' Lise said slowly, 'it's because of something they believe in.'

'But what good does it do getting yourself killed? I mean, if you believe in it, then do something about it.'

Lise shivered again. The salty tang of the stockfish and garlic lingered in her mouth. 'I've been thinking. About what you did. Raymond.' She swallowed. 'You were right. Thank you.'

'No, I wasn't right. I should have let Fatso do whatever he wanted. What I did just made it worse. Made him angrier. It's no good trying to help people. Especially me. I can't help myself, let alone other people. I just make things worse. Like your pa said, everything I touch goes rotten. I should have left old Ray bloke to it.'

Lise swallowed. 'Then what would have happened to me?'

'You've got to learn, kids like you, you've got to take it from big pustules like that, take whatever he dishes out. That's the way of the world. There's no magic rescue.'

'You're not as bad as you make out.'

He sat back and folded his arms. 'Oh no?'

'You worked all day today.'

'Like someone said to me once, that's one day, what about the rest of your life? It's easy for you, you do little sins, little wrong things, you hit your sister, you think a bad thought, you go to Father Robideau, he hears you out, he loves it, all the little girl sins, it makes his mouth water, then he gives you penance. It's easy. For you. But me, there's no point, it doesn't matter how many afternoons I spend scraping out milk churns, putting wheels back on barrows. It won't make any difference.'

'What have you done that's so bad?'

He looked away

Her heart swelled up inside her. 'You can tell me. I won't tell anyone.' She reached out and touched his shoulder. He pushed himself to his feet, scuffing and kicking and slapping at things as he spoke. His eyes were dark, and he wasn't smiling. 'I lied to you.'

'What about?'

He faced her, a snarly smile on his face, as though he was enjoying hurting her, and himself.

'Remember my ma?'

'Yes.'

'I told you about when she died.'

'Yes, the bomb, the house –'

'It wasn't like that.'

Lise's chest went icy. 'She's not dead?'

'Oh, she's dead, but I wasn't there.'

'Where were you?'

His eyes darted here and there, anywhere but to meet hers. 'She threw me out last summer, nearly a year ago. Cos I was always getting into trouble. So she told me to get out, but I wouldn't, then one day she changed the lock on the door, and that was it. So I lived the whole winter in the streets. Until I got caught.' He met her eyes again. 'Arrested. For stealing.' His face was still set in a kind of smile. 'So when she got killed, I was in detention, in the youth custody place at

Cambrai. The priest came and told me. Nice chap. And I never told her I loved her, and I never said goodbye. You know the last thing I said to her?'

Lise shook her head.

'Eff off, you stupid cow. That's what I said to her. I shouted it at her through the letterbox, the day she changed the locks. Then I spat on the door.'

Lise blinked, her stomach churning, clinging on. Her voice came out mechanical. 'But you're sorry now.'

'Sorry? Maybe. But I tell you this. The Germans attacking, it was the best thing that could have happened for me.'

'Why?'

'They had to let us out. In case the bombs hit the custody place. They let us all out, and told us where to report, but I didn't go. I legged it. Cos I can't stand it, being cooped up, locked up. And if they catch me now, they'll lock me up all right. Throw away the key.' He squirmed his shoulders, stopped, picked up the martyr book, fingered it. 'I'm leaving. I wasn't going to tell you. I can't stand it here.'

Silence. Jaq darted his head this way and that, uneasy, glancing up at her, looking away.

Like he's waiting, Lise thought, *for me to say – what?* It was as though she was looking at some copy, some fake, some doll.

She steadied herself. 'If you want me to hate you, I can't. If you want me to make it easy for you, I won't. If you want to go, go, but no one's making you, no one's forcing you. It's your decision.'

She turned to go.

'Wait! That's not all.'

Lise turned slowly back. She felt like a statue, made of some heavy clay stuff.

He knelt, prised away at a floorboard with his thin fingers. The floorboard lifted. He reached in, pulled out something silver, put it on the floor: the missing salt cellar.

Lise's voice was flat. 'You took it?'

He squirmed his shoulders. Nodded. 'I don't know why. It's useless. I saw it. It's like everything. I see something, next thing, it's in my bag. It's not like a decision, I don't say, oh I'll take that. One minute it's there, and the next minute –'

He broke off, and shook his head.

'It's not just that –'

The door creaked. A flicker of yellow light sent the shadows jumping.

Maman.

Lise stood up quickly.

'It's late,' said Yvette.

'My fault,' said Jaq. 'I kept her talking.' He had the salt cellar in his hands, guilty, half-concealed.

Yvette Durelle lifted the candle. Her pale face shone. She looked for a moment at the salt cellar. 'There's no harm in talking.' Her quiet voice filled the room, spreading to the corners, steadying the shadows. 'We're as ready as we can be.' She stooped to kiss Lise. Jaq watched, tense. Yvette turned to him. He stood, rigid, the salt cellar in his hands like a Wise Man with a gift. 'Thank you,' Yvette said, 'for all your help today.'

Far away came Lottie's little voice. 'Maman, Maman, where are you, I feel sick.'

Yvette put the candle on the small table. 'Goodnight,' she said, 'I'll leave you to it.'

The door shut behind her.

Jaq sat down, still holding the salt cellar. 'Why didn't she say anything?'

'Maybe she didn't notice.'

'She saw, and she knows. And you know the worst thing?'

Lise shook her head.

'I've got the pepper too.'

Suddenly there was a barking outside, and Robert burst into the room. Ran to the window, pointed. 'Look, the barn!'

Chapter Twenty-two

They run outside. A flame has caught old hay against the barn wall. It smokes and flares. Jaq wrestles free the door latch, and creaks the door open, and out flies Malcio, yelping and bounding to Lise. Robert picks up the slosh bucket, flings the water at the fire. For a moment the flame sputters, then burns back fiercer.

'The hose tap!' Jaq shouts. 'Turn it on.'

Grande Tante stumbles out, chamberpot in hand.

Lise runs along the path to the tap. Robert follows, grabs the green hose, and pulls and tugs it. Jaq meets him halfway and takes the nozzle.

Lise struggles with the hard metal of the tap. Stuck.

'Be quick,' urges Grande Tante, flinging her pot load on to the sizzling flames.

Robert pants back, puts his hands over Lise's.

'Come on!' he shouts. Straining. Bruising her fingers. They both wrench at the tap. It gives with a clunk. The hose still lies limp along the ground.

'The tank, must be blocked again,' Lise shouts.

Jaq throws the slack hose down, and set off up the slope, Robert scrambling after him.

Maman comes out the kitchen, carrying Lottie. She glances quickly round. The flames are jumping up, along the barn wall, licking towards the house.

'Don't just stand there,' scolds Grande Tante, stumbling out with a skillet.

Struggling up the hill, Jaq glances back. Pretty, the orange flames, spreading in leaps along the barn wall. Can see Lise, still standing with the hose, waiting.

The tank, and the inspection cover. He shouts to Robert, 'Give us a hand, someone's wedged it.'

Together they heave the block of concrete away. 'Try and get a grip on the edge,' urges Jaq.

The rusty plate rasps, then shifts. Jaq stands back. Robert covers his mouth. Staring up at them are the blank milky eyes of a dead sheep.

Yvette threw another spadeful of dirt at the flames. The fire sucked and gasped, hot on their faces. Lise still held the hose. Malcio jumped round her, ears flat, yelping.

Grande Tante struggled out of the cowbarn, leading the two cows. 'We'll have to leave it,' she shouted, 'or we'll all be fried.'

Yvette turned, called to Lise. 'Come on, it's too late, we've got to go.'

Lise glanced up the hill, the flames blinding her. A section of the barn wall crumbled, and smoke sucked into the black gap.

Maman runs across the yard, pulls Lise by the arm. 'Come on!' Yanks the hose out of her hands, throws it down. As the nozzle hit the ground, it reared, then stiffened with the surge of water, writhing and spraying. Maman and Lise fall on it, grappling with it, trapping the hose under their arms, and the water arches out. The flames dance, but there's no escape.

The air is singed, charred, heavy with the dampening.

'It could have been an accident,' Yvette said, carrying Lottie quickly back into the house.

Lottie coughed, and snivelled. 'Thirsty.'

Grande Tante took her, sat down, cooing. Yvette went to the sink.

'No!' Robert steps in, holding out his filthy hands. 'This mouldy old sheep, we pulled it out of the tank.'

'No wonder the water's been off,' said Grande Tante.

From the ruins of the barn, Malcio was whimpering.

Robert turned to Lise. 'Can't you shut him up?'

'In a minute.' Lise sat herself on a big kitchen chair, wrapped a blanket round her shoulders. Shivering, teeth chattering. Looked at Maman. So pale, in the candlelight, eyes hollow.

'There, there,' said Grande Tante, stroking Lottie's hair.

Lottie shivered. 'What happens if they come again?'

Grande Tante waved her pinking shears. 'They'll get more than they bargained for, don't you fret.'

Yvette handed Lottie a tumbler of juice. Looked round. 'Where's Jaq?'

Chapter Twenty-three

The night pitch-black, cool. Jaq forced himself up and over the metal gate. He whistled very quietly, just a breath of a whistle at his lips. He tried to feel that good feeling, the moving on feeling, on to a new tomorrow, forget the past, cut it loose. The rucksack sat on his back.

His pace quickened. He ran, stepping and hopping and jumping over the potholes. With each step, a tug, a pang.

He felt at the inside pocket of his jacket. Something bulged. A little velvet pouch. It burnt next to his heart. Sweat broke out under Jaq's armpits.

He hurried on.

'You owe them nothing,' he said, out loud. Then, in his head: 'And even if you do owe them something, who cares?' And he tried to sneer to himself. But, it felt sour.

'Let go, let go, let go!' he hissed.

And leapt on down the path, leapt on as though trying to avoid grasping hands, tentacles of love and connection.

* * *

Lise pushed open the door of the small parlour. Put the candle lamp carefully on the dresser.

The room was empty, and as neat as if Jaq had never been there. The floorboard was back in place. In the middle of the floor lay the book of martyrs, and next to it something wrapped in a yellow duster. Lise picked up the book. It was open at St Dismas. Picture of a skinny man with a halo hanging on a cross. 'St Dismas, the patron saint of thieves.' Dismas grinned ghoulishly at her. He had a shaved head, and his eyes were big. She put the book down quickly, felt at the duster. Something wrapped. Picked it up. Heavy. Pinned to it was a scrap of paper, scrawled in childish letters, the as back to front: 'In case you think I'm any good.'

Slowly, Lise slipped the duster away.

Found herself staring at a cheap crucifix.

Old and ugly, poorly made, chipped wood, rusty metal. Jesus had no eyes, no face, really.

Her hands are shaking. Her stomach, whirling, a tornado of rage. Wants to throw it, sling it, smash it.

She crept back into the kitchen.

Grande Tante and Lottie have gone. Just Maman, asleep, her face on her arm, slumped over the table. Her mouth was open. Lise touched her arm. Maman started, woke, her head jerked off her hands. She spoke quickly, blinked, as though confused.

'Lottie's not very well, I think it's the water, she's going to sleep in with Grande Tante. We've got some water in the barrel, I think it's clean, maybe in the morning Jaq can go over to the well –'

Lise stood straight. 'No.'

Maman looked puzzled. Scared. Anxious. And for a moment Lise saw her, not as a woman, but as a child. Lise clenched her fists. 'He's gone.'

Maman started. 'Are you sure?'

'He left a note.'

'What did it say?'

Lise hesitated. 'It was addressed to me.'

Maman nodded quickly, looked away. 'Of course. Well, a strange time to go, but that's his choice, I wish him well –'

And then her jaw started to shudder, and her face dropped on to her hands, her shoulders heaved, and she was crying.

Lise stood, her hand half-stretched towards her mother's shoulders. Shoulders heaving like the world heaving, Maman, who never, ever cried, always calm, always able, now, the whole world heaving and shuddering with her slender shoulders. Touch Maman's shoulder, touch the end of the world, the end of childhood.

Under the thin dress, the strap was tight.

'Don't cry,' Lise said.

Under her hand the shuddering shoulder calmed like a big horse settling.

'We'll be fine,' Lise whispered, her lip twitching, voice

catching, an ache back in the nose, but not crying.

Maman stood up and went quickly to the sideboard. Keeping her back to Lise, blew her nose, straightened her hair. Then turned. 'Whatever happens,' she said, 'I'm so proud of you.'

Then she turned away again, and Lise turned too, and walked slowly out, and up the dark stairs, and into her empty bedroom.

The hut loomed grey in the moonlight.

'Giuseppe?' The name croaked strange in Jaq's mouth. He listened. Frogs groaned lower down the slopes. Jaq looked around. Tried the door. It was padlocked and chained. But the hinges were rusty and battered. Jaq felt in his bag, took out a screwdriver and set to work.

He tried to steady his hand. The driver wouldn't stay in the screw's groove.

Jaq felt in the bag again. The tyre lever. He slid the flat end under the hinge, then yanked up. The screws gave with a rasp. Jaq lifted the door open, balanced it, and ducked into the lean-to.

So much stuff.

No one's got big enough pockets.

For a moment he was paralysed.

Could see himself, from the outside, standing there with all this stuff he didn't want, he didn't need, could see himself like Lise, like Madame would see him.

Then he pulled a floppy tool bag off the wall, and working with quick movements, started to stuff it with booty: chisels, saws, nails, drills, a set of bits, a big flashlight, a length of rope – good for the mountains. A silver whistle – like the police use. Nice.

The bag began to bulge.

What we really want is some stashed treasure.

What's this, under the work bench?

A big metal toolbox. Jaq dragged it out.

Cash'll do nicely.

He flipped the lid open. Reached carefully in. The pistol fitted snug in his hand, the metal cool. Not just one pistol, four of them, old-fashioned, army looking, dark metal. And a bag, what? Lumpy, heavy. He reached in. Pulled out a metal sphere, knobbled, with a metal loop on the end. *Hand grenade.*

A shiver shot up his back.

Outside, the scuffling of feet.

Jaq shut the box, and crouched.

Giuseppe?

No.

Cocky voices. Drunk? Laughing. A swagger.

'That'll teach them!'

'I hope they like a bit of mutton with their water!'

'Roast mutton!'

'Where next?'

'Hey, that's that old Itie's hut, ain't it?'

'Reckon so.'

'That could do with a bit of fire treatment as well.'

And the voices crowed agreement.

Feet crunched across the yard.

Jaq pressed himself back against the wall. In his hand, he still held the grenade.

Outside the door, a clanking, and then the ghastly smell of petrol.

Jaq eeled himself across the hut. The one window was blind with grime. Frantically he fingered at the catch, trying to shift it.

'Who's got a light?'

'Here we go.'

A band of yellow light picked out the door, the shelves. Jaq squirmed under the bench.

'Here, the door's off its hinges.'

'Let's have a look inside –'

The torch beam wavered nearer.

Jaq put the grenade to his mouth, teeth on the pin.

'Hang on! Here comes the Itie himself.'

The torch beam disappeared.

Jaq slithered his way to the door. He peered out into the gloom. No sign of the men.

But, someone approaching along the track: cautious, ducking his head, in and out of the shadows. The warning choked in Jaq's throat. Not ten metres away, the first shadow flung itself on Giuseppe.

There was a scrambling, oaths, scuffling, and then the torch flapped on again, and they had him. One man on either arm, another in front. Giuseppe struggled, crouching, pulling, snarling at them.

'Come on,' shouted the torch-man. 'Swear. Swear your loyalty to France.'

'Say it, say "I love France".'

'Say "Italy's the dregs".'

Giuseppe lunged and twisted, and for a moment he was free, sprawling on the ground. The torch beam swung wildly. Then the torch-man caught Giuseppe with a boot in the ribs, and the others were on him again, fiercer, punching, kicking, pulling him out of Jaq's line of sight.

'I told you he was a traitor.'

'Come clean.'

'Come on!'

'Admit you're a spy.'

Another thud, and a groan.

Jaq's fists clenched and unclenched. The breath was tight and painful in his throat. *Your chance to get away.* Slowly, carefully, he swung the heavy bag full of booty on to his shoulder.

Outside, a clink and rattle.

'Try this.'

A ripping sound.

'Hold him.'

A swish, and a slap, and a sob.

Jaq leaned his head further and peered into the darkness.

The torch was on the ground, the torch-man had a belt. Giuseppe's shirt had been torn away, the two men held him so his bare back faced the torch-man. He swung the belt again, so the buckle caught Giuseppe on the ribs. Giuseppe jerked, and swore.

Jaq exploded out of the hut. As he went, he hauled the bench over, so cans and nails and tools and weights came crashing down. He shoved the door, blew the whistle, zapped on the flashlight, swung his arm.

The men froze.

Something rolled across the hard ground, bobbling.

'Grenade!' shouted one, and the men threw themselves into the bushes.

Jaq ran.

Headlong, down the path, throat on fire. Flat out, full speed, the bag dragging him backwards, downwards.

Chapter Twenty-four

Lise can't sleep.

Without Lottie, the room seems bare. The dark has sharp edges. *He's out there somewhere.*

Hanging in her head too, that stupid dream she's played over every night since he came. The dream of living rough, on the streets, making do and keeping warm, hiding, begging, stealing – no, they don't steal, they work, and buy their food, and save enough to buy a little cottage. Anything'll do, even a hut like Giuseppe's. They mend it, and make it snug, and get the fire going. Have a dog. And chickens, of course. And she helps Jaq so he doesn't hurt people any more, and doesn't have to lie, and she teaches him so he can do his exams, and then he goes to university, and gets a really good job, and he sits at table with Papa, and they discuss serious things, and everyone likes him.

She squirms again, rolls over, buries her face. So stupid. The glow's all gone. It's all too real. *You're on your own.*

Lise tries to find some good thing to think about. But the images glare back at her, harsh and real: Papa, Raymond, flames, girls at school, tanks in a field, Maman's shoulders heaving, heaving . . .

That's not all.

There's something else, downstairs, under a floorboard, wrapped in a duster, a heavy awkward cheap thing, and it prods, goads, makes her shift and squirm.

Anger and misery, boiling in her chest.

Jaq, why did you have to come here?

She rolls over, forces her forehead against the cool plaster of the wall.

No use.

With a curse, she throws off the covers.

The moon has set behind the mountain.

Whoever invented mountains wants his head examined. Jaq crouched among the rocks, looked around. That must be Italy, over there. Every path he'd followed had taken him somewhere he didn't want to go. That peak, up there, it looks like you can reach out and touch it. It looks like you've climbed as high as you can climb. But then the path you're on disappears, or you come to a sheer drop, or a wall of trees and brush so thick you need a steamroller to get through it.

The blessed bag's getting heavier and heavier.

Now, he pushes off again, edging along the narrow track

cut into the side of the slope. Is he heading into Italy, or back towards France?

The climb gets steeper.

Tired.

Jaq dozed. The sky was sharp blue inside his eyelids, and every time he dropped off, a shudder of bombs in his head shook him awake.

Then he dreamed of Lise, Madame, the fire – and he snapped awake again. He clutched at his shirt. The pouch. Still there.

A big cat came prowling, wants to eat him . . .

Then he realised, he'd woken from one dream into another. Paralysed. Arms trapped by his sides.

The cat's prowling, can't get away. Can't even open his mouth to scream – the cat flies up into the sky, ready to dive –

The dream began to clank and growl. Buckets clanged round his head, and grinning men chanted. Then he woke up, again. Voices. Close. Cheerful, shouting in whispers.

This is real.

They're talking Italian.

The grey light of just-before-dawn.

The narrow road was lined with trucks, round the bend in both directions. Towards the head of the column were light, tracked vehicles, with armour plating and large machine guns. Towards the rear was a neat stack of bicycles, and several mules with their noses in foodbags.

Jaq reached down, rubbed his fingers in the dirt, and smeared it on to his face. Then bent double, with a quick glance each way, he trotted out from behind the rocks and across the road. He darted between two trucks, and then slithered down the slope on the other side.

Seemed as though no one had seen him. Then a shout.

'Hey, you, where are you going?'

'Stop, or I fire.'

'No, don't shoot,' hissed an officer, 'it'll give away our position.'

Jaq crashed down the slope, and the soldiers crashed down after him. He broke through on to the mule path. Which way? Who knows? He darted left. The path swung round the edge of the hill, and there far, far below was the darkness of the sea. Behind, the soldiers swore, their boots pounding, scuffing on the hard ground.

Jaq stopped. The path ahead crumbled away into nothing.

'Got him!' shouted the officer.

Jaq didn't hesitate. He dropped the rucksack and leapt, sliding feet first down the steep slope. For twenty metres he managed to keep control, then his foot catches a rock, and now he's half-sliding, half-falling, helplessly, faster and faster, with a sudden thud which knocks all the air out of him, he lands in a thick patch of – what?

Above, the soldiers peer down into the gloom.

'Don't give much for his chances,' said one.

'What do you reckon he was up to?'

'Lost probably.'

'There's his bag.'

The sergeant picked it up. 'Heavy!' Opened it, pulled out the rope. 'Is he a boy scout, or what?'

'More likely a spy.'

Lise struggled up the path. She moved quickly, driven by a fury in the pit of her stomach. Under her arm she clasped the bundle. Heavy, getting heavier. The wind plastered her dress against her, and a misty rain soaked her hair. Past the water tank. Up to the brow. *Pigache land.* Who cares? Let them all come, and their dogs, and their hoods, and their torches. She'll fight them, kill them. Or be killed.

She stopped on the height of the cliff. Far below, the hissing of the sea seemed to suck her towards it.

Angrily, cursing under her breath, Lise pulled the duster away, held the naked crucifix. *Why did you come here? I hope you rot in hell.*

Then she wound her arm back, and flung the crucifix up and out so it spun down and crashed, hopping from rock to rock until with a final, silent splash it disappeared into the sea.

She stood, not breathing, frozen. Inside, she was empty. As though her soul had gone bouncing down with it.

Gone. Got rid of him. Serves you right for caring.

But that's not right. Not true. Inside, the feeling's coming back. As though a thousand demons are crawling out, teeming up through her body like termites, scratching and biting, eating at her. Jaq's face is looming up in her head, grinning at her, wicked, and a voice – Father Robideau? chanting, chanting: 'My child, what have you done?'

As though a thousand searchlight beams are piercing her to the core, and everyone can see her, the wickedness, and nothing left, no shred of hope to cling on to.

The sea swished, sucking at her. She took an unsteady step towards the edge. Felt light, brittle, like a dried thing, all the life parched out.

The sea fizzed and flickered.

I feel so light, I wonder if I'll fly?

And she took another step closer to the edge.

Jaq shook his head. Stench. Animals? Felt with one hand. Soft, slimy, wet. *You've landed in a forage heap.* What's that noise? Swishing. He raises his head. *Surely, it's the sea?*

Jaq tenses. Voices, getting closer.

'He must have killed himself.'

'If he's dead, why haven't we found him?'

Jaq eased himself off the heap. The movement stirred the stench, made him retch. He wormed his way away from the voices, towards the sea. But, a hundred metres further on, he had to stop again. Trucks growling, clanking. Another road.

Jaq blinked in the early light, trying to work it out.

This was the coastal road. It twisted, and then disappeared

into a tunnel in the rock. A queue of trucks and tanks waited at the mouth of the tunnel, which was guarded by dozens of soldiers.

The soldiers were Italians. So, this end of the tunnel is Italy, the other end France.

You've crossed the border.

And a fat lot of good it's done you.

The two soldiers are getting closer, walking casually, one lights a cigarette. Voices loud in the night air.

'What if he is a spy? You don't need a spy to see all this lot.'

Jaq huddled himself under a tree. Leg? All right. Just bruises, scratches, sore. But . . . no bag. No rope, no tools. No coat. *Even down here near the sea, it's chilly.* Up in the mountains, you'll freeze.

Quickly, he worked his way, crouching, along the ditch beside the road. *Got to take chances, now.* Ahead, a barrier, with guards. On both sides of the road, fences, high fences with barbed wire. Another truck rumbled past. Jaq flattened himself, then jumped up, and darted across the road behind the truck. *Find a hole in the fence – or make one.*

He hurried along the line of the fence, keeping his distance. Every hundred metres, a sentry. *Hopeless – unless.*

That tree. Climb that, throw yourself.

He ducked his way to the tree. The sentry turned slowly, stared, made no move. Jaq reached up, found the branch, swung himself up.

'Halt, who goes there?'

A flashlight burned out, turning the whole area vivid white and black.

Yvette was nearly asleep. In her head a big moth with dark eyes was butting its ugly head against a lantern, trying to knock it over, and set the house on fire.

She woke, startled.

What?

It was as though the back end of a thunderclap was hanging in her head.

She lay stiff and on guard. Something missing? Georges. She shivered. Blinked away the flames, the stares of the market women, the rancid water, Lottie's feverish face. Slowly the darkness floated up like water seeping into blotting paper –

CRACK!

The sky outside flared orange.

Yvette flew to the window. The sky was fading, but the echo of the explosion still boomed and crackled in the air.

Jaq hung from the tree.

And then the ground seemed to buck under him. Out of the tunnel shot a tube of grey smoke, and a scattering of rock and splinters. Then the explosion. The shock of it hit him like a sudden flat hand in the chest, and threw him down on to the ground. The sentry, he was down too. Jaq picked himself up and sprinted flat out towards the sea.

* * *

Lise cowered back into the rocks, paralysed. *What was it?* She'd fallen, clung to a clump of brush. Then the sound, so low it shuddered in your belly. She sat up, staring round. The sea seemed suddenly big, and heavy, nasty. She scrambled further away from the edge.

Again, the sky to the east lit up orange, and moments later the shudder. Lise jumped up, and ran.

Chapter Twenty-five

At last, the sea. Jaq knelt, took several deep breaths. Ahead, a ramshackle jetty. In the gloom before dawn a few boats bobbed in the water. The tackle clinked at the mastheads.

Light beginning to seep up in the east.

Jaq ran on to the jetty. The loose boards clattered.

The wallowing boat bucked and slid as Jaq stepped into it. The bottom was wet. He cut the rope with two sharp strokes of his knife, and pushed away from the jetty.

Cold.

Wet. Bottom of the boat, filling, was it?

The wind whipped up stronger.

Above, the stars are dying one by one, eaten by the blueing sky.

Jaq pulled the last crust of bread out of his shirt. Chewed. Gulped. A plane clanked and roared overhead.

Where now?

Vague in his head, the map. How far? Is there a tide, or

a current? He slotted the oars into the rowlocks, and began to row.

Lise ran down the track.

It was raining now, big drops of rain, plopping on the trees.

The path was damp.

At the bottom of the track she hesitated.

Should she take the road or the path?

Every bush, every tree, loomed like a threat.

The path. It was shorter, and more cover.

She pushed on through the trees.

Her feet seemed to make so much noise on the carpet of needles and leaves and dust. Everything was so quiet, close-to, as though the animals and insects had been cowed by the huge explosions.

The path got narrower.

Lise trotted faster.

Of course she wasn't lost. Of course this was the right path.

A bush loomed as though it had moved on purpose to block and confuse her. Something scuttled off to the side. Something else hissed. Rain dropped and plopped and slid from the branches above.

Lise stopped. Her heart was bulging. Her throat was sore. Above she could make out the vague looming shape of the mountain. She cursed.

Too far to the east. Work back west.

She struck off to her left, up the slope. But the bushes got thicker, they pulled at her, brambles and briars and thorns. She looked up, and there was the mountain again.

You're going in the wrong direction.

Panic. Her thoughts scattered. She swallowed down her fear.

Deep breaths.

Shivered. A noise. What? Trickling.

The stream. Follow that, you're safe.

She stopped.

Something there, by the stream. An animal? Hunched. Washing? Lise tried to move away, slowly. Her dress snagged on a branch. The crack sounded loud as an explosion. The shape jerked round. Bare torso, face bruised, bloody.

'Giuseppe!' Lise gasped.

He crouched over to her, eyes wild, took her arm, shook her.

'What you do? What you do? It's dangerous out here.'

Lise sniffed. 'Couldn't sleep.'

He spat, let her go, glanced all round. 'It isn't safe.'

'Those explosions –'

'The French soldiers blow the mountain passes.'

'Why?'

'To stop the Italian soldiers crossing through the tunnels.'

Lise swallowed. 'What happened to you?'

He shook his head. 'Don't matter. Don't tell, all right? Now go. Take care.'

And he touched her arm, and hunched away into the trees.

* * *

Jaq didn't see the town until he was nearly past it. No lights. Only the looming dark shapes of the houses, a church on a hill, and then the faint white of the hotels along the front.

At the harbour mouth the sentries lounged. Ten metres below, the rowing boat slid silently. The water chocked on the bows.

One of the sentries yawned. 'The Italians? They'll never attack us.'

The bow of the boat slid, rasped against the stone harbour wall. Jaq, lying flat, stuck out a foot, and heaved, and the boat slid into the harbour.

'Gone? Has he?' said Grande Tante. 'Check the spoons!'

'He's taken all the bread,' said Yvette, her voice flat, beaten. She sat with head bowed, hands clasped.

Grande Tante frowned, and then laughed. 'What do you expect, from a thief?'

Yvette shook her head. 'I offered to give him food.'

Grande Tante snorted. 'His sort, they prefer to steal it. I hope you kept your valuables locked up.'

Yvette looked away, ran a hand through her hair. 'I'm not sure what else he's taken. It doesn't really matter.' She looked up at Grande Tante. 'Lise has gone too.'

'With him?'

'I don't know. I went to see she was all right after the explosions. Her room's empty.'

Grande Tante shook her head. 'I warned you –'

Yvette looked up. Her eyes were bright. 'I know, you did tell me, and you were right.'

'We all make mistakes,' said Grande Tante.

Yvette stood up. 'I'm not sure what to do.'

Grande Tante waddled over to her. Put her hand on Yvette's shoulder. 'You've done everything you can.'

Lise hobbled in, rubbing her arm.

Yvette swung round, stood straighter. 'Where have you been?'

Lise sat down, shrugged, shivered. 'Malcio, he was whimpering, I went to check he was all right.'

'You've been out there two hours?'

'I fell asleep.'

Yvette sat down, the breath shuddering out through her lips.

Lise snapped at her. 'What does it matter?'

Grande Tante offered Lise half an apple. 'We thought you might have taken off with lover boy.'

'Lover boy? Don't talk rubbish. Why should I go with him? He's nothing but trouble.'

Lottie's voice wailed out from down the hall.

Yvette got up and went out.

Grande Tante shook her head. 'Poor little devil. She was sick in the night, two or three times. And talking nonsense.'

'Do you think it's the water?'

'Either that or the blessed fish.' And Grande Tante belched loudly.

Robert hurried in with the milk churn. 'There's men, down the hill, coming this way.'

Grande Tante struggled to her feet. 'Right. Hoods or no hoods, I'll take care of them.'

'They're not hoods, they're police.'

Yvette sat at the kitchen table. Luffau stood in front of her, rocking on his heels. Grande Tante sat in her chair, Lise and Robert on the window bench. Two military policemen guarded the door.

'The young man, he's gone,' Yvette said. 'We had a fire, last night, he went –'

Luffau raised a hand. 'Please, I know all that. I'm more interested in Giuseppe Villani. Do you know where he is?'

Yvette shook her head.

'Giuseppe?' Grande Tante called from her chair. 'He's mad. A law unto himself.'

Luffau ignored her. Leaned with his knuckles on the table, closer to Yvette. 'You allow him use of a hut, on your land?'

'Yes. He keeps his tools in it.'

'Not just tools. Acting on information received last night, we searched the place and found a stash of weapons. Do you know anything about that?'

Yvette shook her head. 'He was always strange.'

'Strange and it seems dangerous. In league with the fascists.'

'Don't be ridiculous,' Grande Tante scoffed. 'Mad maybe, but a fascist? Never. He comes from right down the toe of

Italy, a wild place. He had it very hard as a boy. He hates the fascists.'

'There is such a thing as a double agent, or sleeper. And it seems very likely that your young thief is in some way mixed up with him. He was seen at the hut by an informant –'

'Who?' demanded Grande Tante.

Luffau smiled. 'The informant was anonymous.'

'Wearing a hood?' scoffed Grande Tante.

Luffau's thick lips twitched. 'In a world such as ours it doesn't matter how we get information. All that matters is that it's accurate, and if it's accurate we act on it.'

Lise swallowed hard. 'And did your informant beat him up?' Luffau turned slowly to look at her. 'How did you know Giuseppe Villani was beaten up?'

Lise closed her mouth.

Luffau took a slow, swaggering step towards her. Lise's fists clenched. Luffau sat himself next to her on the window bench. His arm lay behind her. She could smell him. He stared up at the ceiling. 'My dear, I know you have a warm heart, a soft heart, but now you must realise this isn't like telling tales in school. Giuseppe Villani is a very bad and dangerous man. If you know anything about him, where he is, you must tell me.'

'I saw him. This morning. I don't know where he is now.'

Luffau stood up. He spoke to Lise, but stared at Yvette. 'You see, there are other considerations. For example, no one else round here employed Giuseppe. Only your father.' Now he turned and put a finger under Lise's chin and lifted her face so she had to look at him. 'And, I believe your father has also disappeared. That makes three.'

'My husband went to join up with his old unit.' Yvette stood up. 'Please don't touch my children.'

Luffau took his hand away from Lise's face. 'No doubt that's the story your husband told you, and what you believe. I beg to differ.' He glanced round the kitchen. 'I'm afraid we'll have to search the whole place.'

Chapter Twenty-six

Grey light, turning yellow as the sun heats the air. The edge of town.

Jaq rested for a moment on a crumbling wall, sniffed. Ahead, the alley was cobbled and narrow, a whiff of pee, the houses high all round. Washing hanging. Shuttered windows, large dark heavy doors with brass bolts and bosses. Big rusty hinges. The air was still, and yet tense. A lank dog limped across the cobbles. A gaggle of little children chased an older girl who dragged a doll. They barked like dogs. Bare feet slapping. Big eyes stared at Jaq, run on, away round the corner.

Discarded on a step, a mouth organ.

Jaq stooped.

Above, shutters clattered open. 'What do you want?' A woman, wrestling a feather bed out of the window.

Jaq put his head down and hurried on.

Steps, downwards. Stink of fish. Damp. Jaq hesitated at

the bottom of the steps. A square. A scattering of people, anxious. Metal poles and canvas awnings. Shouts, nervous laughter. The remains, or beginnings of the market.

Dong! Dong! Dong!

The bell of the church, tolling a slow succession of single chimes.

Two women hurry past.

Jaq ducked out of the shadows into the early sunshine. He picked his way among the scattered stalls. Only a few early customers. People shout the latest rumours to each other.

'The passes have all been blown.'

'There's German paratroopers landed in the hills.'

'The Germans are in Paris.'

'Our army's given up.'

'Italy's going to attack us.'

Jaq hesitated at a clothes stall, fingered a thick coat.

'Hey watch it. No buy, no touch, sunshine.'

Suspicious eyes follow Jaq, stallholders nudge each other, question, 'Seen him before?'

Jaq stopped at another stall: toys, tools.

'Excuse me,' Jaq called.

The man looked up. Checked shirt, big hands. 'What?'

Jaq eased the mouth organ out of his pocket. 'You want to buy?'

The man glanced at the mouth organ, then at Jaq. 'Not from your sort, son.'

Jaq's throat tightened. 'What's wrong with my sort?'

'Look at yourself.'

The woman on the next stall called out, 'I bet that's stolen.'

And the woman on the other side, fussing with her rings and bracelets. 'I'd call the marshall, Pierre. That kid smells like a cow pat.'

Jaq slid the mouth organ back into his pocket and hurried on.

Ahead, two policemen, moving purposefully, peering into corners. Pointing our infringements to traders. Refusing to answer anxious questions about the war.

'It's business as usual,' one said.

'What, and no one allowed on the beach?'

Jaq ducked down a side aisle. Came out by the fish market. Trays of bright-eyed fish and mussels, glistening in ice. And beyond these, in a gloomy corner, the last cheap stalls. Here you could buy odds and ends, sad remnants. Jaq huddled himself into a niche in the wall, and watched.

An old couple were trying to sell bits and pieces out of a battered suitcase.

'Our last things, from home, before the bombs.'

The stallholder, a red-faced woman with tattoos, shook her head. 'If you haven't got identity papers, I can't buy.'

Against the fish-market wall, a man was leaning. He was pale, a sickly white, like uncooked suet. Very thin, hunched shoulders, as though he was expecting a griping pain in the stomach. A thin cigarette stuck to his top lip.

'Maybe I can help,' he drawled.

'Clear off, Salacroup, you rogue,' the red-faced woman shouted.

The old man dragged the case over. Salacroup crouched by it. 'Twenty francs the lot.'

'That's robbery!'

Salacroup held out two dirty banknotes. 'Take it or leave it.'

A murmur, then a shout.

Jaq glanced round. The gendarmes. Stepping quicker, their boots clacking on the concrete. The old woman snatched the notes, Salacroup snatched up the case.

Then there was a scurry, and it all happened in a rush. Two more gendarmes, coming the other way, barged into Jaq, he squirmed and swore, but they jostled past him, and a whistle blew, and the gendarmes had hold of the old couple.

The suitcase had gone, and so had Salacroup.

The old man sank to his knees, his head in his hands.

'Black marketeering,' said the gendarme, 'it's a serious offence.'

Luffau threw a notepad down on the table. 'This is your receipt book?'

Yvette glanced, nodded.

'Containing orders from a Corporal Vincenzi of the Italian army?'

'That's right. My husband used to deliver milk to the Italian border troops, until the state of emergency was declared.'

Luffau sighed, shook his head sadly. 'It all fits, and it's all pretty damning. I'm not saying you personally knew anything that was going on. At the very least this constitutes fraternising with the enemy.'

Grande Tante sniffed. 'You've searched the whole house, and that's all you've found. Orders for a quart of cow's milk? I can't see a court making much of that.'

Luffau turned on her. 'Madame, one would hardly expect a nest of spies and fifth columnists to leave incriminating evidence lying around in the open. No. I'm sure there's more to be found, if only we knew where to look.'

Again he glanced round the room. His eyes fell on Robert. Robert squirmed on his chair. Luffau leaned over him. 'You must have been pals with the thief, lad. Did he have any secret hiding places, that kind of thing?'

Robert shook his head. 'He didn't like me. He never told me anything.'

'How about your charming sister?'

Lise straightened her shoulders. Shook her head. 'He didn't leave anything, he never had anything.'

Luffau leaned closer. His eyes were bright behind the tortoiseshell glasses. He seemed so confident, so friendly, as though he knew everything already. 'Young lady, it will go very badly for you if you're lying –'

Lise shook her head again, her lips tight.

Luffau tutted, softly. 'Such a pity, if I have to take you down to the Gendarmerie for interrogation.'

The door swung open. Lottie, face pale, cheeks burning red, her eyes red-rimmed, hair messed. 'I know where he hides things,' she said.

Lise gripped the arms of her chair.

Luffau smiled. 'Come, my dear, and show us.'

Jaq followed Salacroup. It wasn't easy. The man darted into a small lane. Up steps, turn left, turn right. Narrower and narrower. Damp and dark, the sky a thin line of blue high above.

Under an arch, round another corner.

Jaq stopped. Salacroup, where was he?

A sour sleeve snaked round Jaq's neck and dragged him backwards.

'Why are you following me?'

Jaq wrenched himself round, so he could see the pale, sickly face. 'I've got stuff to sell.'

The arm loosened.

Salacroup pointed to a set of narrow filthy steps leading down into a basement. 'Follow me, and no tricks.'

Luffau knelt on the floor of the small parlour. The floorboard lay beside him. In front of him a neat line of objects: a candlestick, a photo frame, a clock.

'Those are his things,' Lise said. 'His mother's things. Her last things, before she was killed.'

Luffau weighed a candlestick in his hand. 'Young lady,

these things you touchingly describe as his mother's are almost certainly stolen from a variety of places in a trail right down through France.'

Luffau reached again into the cavity. Felt around, frowning. Stopped. Pulled out a leather case.

'What's this?' he demanded.

'My husband's field glasses,' said Yvette.

Luffau stood up. 'I think that's all we need.'

Yvette shook her head. 'Why? What do you mean? They were missing before he went back to join his unit.'

Luffau brandished the binocular case. 'Clearly there was a stash of military equipment under these floorboards. Your husband, Giuseppe, the thief, they've cleared it – or thought they had, but they've forgotten this one incriminating item.'

Luffau put the case carefully into his satchel. 'You know, Madame Durelle, this could be very serious for you, for all of you. We need to get to the bottom of it. I must ask you not to leave this property until further notice.'

'What about the evacuation?'

'When and if, when and if, Madame Durelle. Personally, I don't think the Italians have got the stomach for a fight, but we'll see. Good day.'

Jaq licked his lips.

So far, so good.

Salacroup lit a candle. The sickly yellow light seeped around the tiny kitchen. Everything damp, chipped, rusty.

No window. A doorway to the rear, covered with a nailed-up blanket.

Jaq and the man eyed each other.

Salacroup's cheek twitched. 'What have you got?'

Jaq hesitated then felt inside his shirt.

'There.'

He carefully placed the green velvet pouch on the table. Watched with distaste as Salacroup's long thin fingers clawed at the drawstring. On to the table tumbled a brooch afire with blue stones, and a ring with a single diamond.

Salacroup held the ring up to the light and squinted at it. 'Initials, Y.D.'

A sick feeling spread in Jaq's stomach. Salacroup sighed. 'I suppose this belonged to some lovely lady. Precious. Engagement, looks like. Token of love. Poor woman. Y.D., must be her name – Ysobel? Yvette?'

'It's family,' Jaq snarled.

Salacroup put the ring down on the table. 'That's right, someone else's family. Or why would you try and sell it to a rogue like me? Why not take it to a proper jeweller in town?'

'A thousand francs,' Jaq said.

Salacroup made a face. 'Maybe. Maybe eight hundred.' He glanced behind him. 'Vaubin?'

A short man in a waistcoat pushed out through the blanket from the rear of the basement. Balding, grubby, thick glasses. Salacroup offered him the pouch. 'Have a look at these, will you?'

Vaubin reached in his waistcoat pocket and drew out an eyeglass.

'My expert,' said Salacroup. 'Take particular note of the ring.'

Vaubin shook his head. 'I need more light.'

Salacroup glanced at Jaq. Jaq hesitated, nodded. Vaubin gathered the pouch, and hunched his way out the back.

Salacroup clasped his long fingers, unclasped them.

Jaq glanced round the kitchen again.

Filth. Just like home.

He shivered. *Something gnawing inside him.*

The big old clock ticked, big lurching ticks.

Salacroup picked at his teeth with his thumbnail.

In Jaq's stomach, a chaos of rage swelling, gathering up into his chest. He clenches and unclenches his fists. *What have you done?*

Salacroup tapped his fingers on the table.

Jaq swallowed. 'I've changed my mind.'

Salacroup's head twitched on his neck. 'What about?'

'That stuff, I want it back, it's not for sale.'

'I'm afraid it's too late for that.'

Jaq stood up. 'Don't mess with me.'

'We made a deal. You can't back out.'

'We never made a deal.'

Salacroup leaned forward. 'The deal is this. I keep the stuff and you clear off.'

Jaq's hand closed over Salacroup's. 'Old man, you've got a long thin neck.'

Salacroup jerked away. In his hand was a knife. He glanced at the old clock on the mantlepiece. 'I'd say you've got a couple of minutes, before the police get here.'

There was a loud hammering on the door, shouts.

'Tough,' twitched Salacroup. 'You should have gone when you had the –'

Jaq threw himself across the room. The table clattered over. Salacroup flinched away. Jaq tore through the blanket, into the rear. Dark. A tiny room, a bed – a window. Stepped up on to the bed, swung his elbow. The glass shattered, and he scrambled out.

Chapter Twenty-seven

Picard licked his pencil. 'So, Monsieur Salacroup, you've turned honest all of a sudden?'

Salacroup put his hand on his heart. 'I've always supported law and order and the free market.'

'And this young man, he tried to steal – what from you?'

'Who knows. He broke in, I surprised him Vaubin ran to fetch you.'

Picard shut his notebook and stood up. 'Pity you didn't manage to detain him.'

The door shut behind him.

Salacroup beckoned to Vaubin with a twitchy grin. 'Come on, let's have a look at the stuff.'

Vaubin reached into his inmost pocket. Reverently pulled out the pouch. 'Worth five grand, at least.'

Salacroup took the pouch. 'Better make sure it's kept safe, then.'

* * *

Jaq raced down the alley, under a bridge, some steps. *Where?* Behind him, whistles. People staring, pointing, shouting. *Need to hide*. Round a corner. Road clogged with people. Cows. Chickens in cages, a pig grunting in the gutter. One policeman directing this way, another that. An engine whistles. The eggy smell of smoke and steam. The train station. A voice blares on a tannoy. 'Please keep calm, the order to evacuate has not yet been given.'

Jaq wriggled himself through the crush. People swore and threatened and pushed.

'Your papers, if you please.'

Gendarme.

Jaq ran.

Into the crowd, vaulting, barging, pushing. A dog snapped at him. The gendarme blew a whistle. Jaq sprawled over a wire fence, dangling down on to tennis courts. Two men were unrolling barbed wire. Jaq jogged past them, and up the slope on the far side.

Lise jumped the draughtsman. 'Your move.'

Lottie shuddered. 'Not playing any more.'

Lise lifted the board and the draughtsmen slid this way, that way. A couple fell on the bed. 'Ow! That hurt!' whined Lottie.

Lise stood up. Clacked the draughtsmen back into the box. The sun was shining. Her chest was tight with fear. Inside, she was empty. As though she'd blanked it all out, the swirling thoughts, the rage, the despair. The crucifix? So what?

Papa, somewhere. Jaq, somewhere. Corporal Vincenzi. And hidden in the folds of the mountains, in among the trees, hundred and hundreds of soldiers.

The clock gonged. Quarter-to.

The church was gloomy. Smelt of wax and incense and candles. The walls were panelled with brown stained wood. Saints and angels loomed down from the walls and ceiling. Huge candles burned in one corner, the candles people light for the sick or dying or dead. The floor was paved with pale pink and yellow tiles.

Wedged into a corner by the lectern, Jaq wriggled his shoulders and chewed at his fingers. Took deep breaths. *Think straight.* The sick feeling lurched up again in his stomach.

Fool, fool, fool.

You let that slimy villain Salacroup make a fool out of you. *But that's not it.* Not why the anger's crawling all up your chest and your head's squirming like scorpions.

It's cos you let him touch Madame's things.

Put his paws –

You let that monster put his dirty fingers –

Jaq shivered. And now Salacroup's got her ring, grinning all over his face, holding it up to the light, slipping it on and off his dirty fingers –

You are worthless, worthless, worthless.

For several moments Jaq hugged himself, and wallowed in

it, in the awfulness of being who he was. It was almost a pleasure, to feel so bad, so utterly bad and worthless that he could never possibly do anything good.

She helped you, and you stole her things.

He caught the blind stare of an angel carved on the seat-end, and jerked away.

Forget it, forget it, forget it.

He studied the pink tiles, forcing himself to make patterns.

The clock gonged the hour. Seven.

Time to go?

What's the point?

Jump a train, get away, Spain, or a boat –

And then it hits him. Cold, clear: what he has to do.

With a growl, he pulls himself to his feet, and crouches towards the door.

Before he got there, the big door creaked open. Jaq froze in the middle of the floor.

The inner door flapped against its frame. Two men, silhouetted in the yellow light of the candles. The shorter of the two removed his hat. They stepped slowly into the nave, looking this way, that way. The taller man wore the habit of a priest. 'And if someone was hiding –' he said.

The shorter man stopped, saw Jaq. 'Well look who we've found.' The light of twenty huge candles glowed on the face of Luffau.

He raised his revolver.

Jaq sprang and vaulted. Cratch! A whine and a crunch.

Jaq slipped and sprawled on his face. The lectern eagle glared over a beakless mess. The shot still boomed in echo. Luffau aimed again.

'For the Lord's sake, not in here!' shouted the priest. Jaq, on knees and feet and hands, slithering on the tiles, squirmed up the altar steps, vaulted the altar, through the vestry door, and out into the sunshine.

Maman switched on the radio. She frowned. Music, blaring. Italian music. She turned the knob. Crackles, then another station. Italian voices, over-loud, excited.

'Where's the news?' demanded Grande Tante.

'That's what I'm trying to get,' Yvette replied, working the dial a little this way, a little that. Every now and then a French voice surfaced for a moment, but before they could make out what it was saying, the Italian stations drowned it. Yvette switched off the radio.

Silence filled the room.

'What's all that in aid of?' asked Grande Tante.

'I'm not sure,' said Yvette, 'but I think we should get away from here.'

Grande Tante frowned. 'The order hasn't been given.'

'Maybe it has, and we don't know.'

Pierre Bernadou hurried out of the town hall. The street was almost deserted. In his arms he carried a large case. Slung it into the back of the red sports car. Two porters staggered out after him, carrying a trunk. Pierre opened the boot, and the porters struggled the trunk in. The boot wouldn't shut.

'Tie it with string,' Pierre said, impatiently.

'I hope that holds,' said the Mayor. 'You've got half the civic records in there.'

Light beginning to fade.

In the town, everything was confusion.

Doors were open.

People running in, out, up the street, down, shouting, calling. Throwing things into boxes and cases, throwing cases on to carts and into prams and wheelbarrows.

Bundles piled on the pavements.

Jaq ran on, back towards the old town.

A mule blocked the way, backing and turning, braying, while its mistress tried to strap a trunk on its back.

A man was struggling with an old pram, trying to get the wheel straight. Jaq stopped. 'What's going on, mate?'

'Give your horse a chance. The order's come through.'

'What for?'

'To evacuate.'

'Why?'

'The Ities, they've declared war.'

Jaq crept down the stairs to Salacroup's basement. Throat tight. Determined. Tried the door.

'Hey, sonny!'

Jaq spun round. Above him, under a crushed black hat, an

old man's toothless face. 'You won't find old Saladcrop at home. He left two hours ago.'

Jaq turned, tried the door again, harder, shaking it. Kicked at it.

'Hey!' said the old man, 'keep on like that and I'll call the police.'

Jaq looked up again. 'He's got something of mine, I need it.'

'Is it worth anything?'

'Sentimental value.'

The old man glanced both ways along the alley, then leaned further over the railings. 'If it's worth a few francs, he'll have flogged it.'

'Where to?'

'What's the merchandise?'

'Jewellery.'

The old man thought for a moment. 'Try the pawn shop on the Rue d'Église.'

Pierre drove down to the Esplanade, and pulled up at the junction by the closed casino. Turn right, for Nice, and safety. Turn left, for the border, and the Domaine. Behind him, a car honked. Pierre glanced back. *All those vital documents, sticking out of the back of the car.*

The car behind honked again.

Yvette, the children, they've probably left already.

With a sigh, Pierre waved a hand to the car behind, and swung the sports car right and on to the road to Nice.

* * *

Now, Jaq was fighting against the tide of people.

Ahead, where the shopping area started, a road block, manned by gendarmes. Jaq edged closer. A man in a waist-coat was arguing with a large gendarme with silver-grey hair.

'But officer Picard, I need to get through,' the man insisted. 'I've got valuable things left there, I can't possibly go without them.'

Officer Picard stood straight. 'I'm sorry, sir, but this area's been cleared and is now under martial law.'

'What if there's looting?'

'We'll take care of that,' replied Picard. 'Anyone crossing this line will be arrested, or shot. And now I'd advise you to clear out as quick as possible. The bombardment could start up any minute.'

Nearly dark.

Jaq dropped down over the fence. The big bins of the butcher's back yard loomed round him. He crouched to the high gate. Listened. Dead silence. Clambered up the gate, swung over, and dropped into the street on the other side.

Deserted.

Behind him, now, the roadblock. Jaq was cautious, on the lookout everywhere. Streets stretch empty.

Heavy boots clumped and clattered on the cobbles. Jaq flattened himself in a doorway. The yellow sweep of a torch beam, and red glows. Soldiers. Smoking furtively. They chatted in whispers. One of them swore, quietly, under his breath. He was old, grey-haired, wrinkled, the other young. Barely out of school, he looked. Their belts and bags squeaked and clinked. Jaq ducked out of the doorway, and darted on down the street.

The shops stood helpless with their big windows all dark, gloomy inside.

Shoe shop. The floor cluttered with a mess of boxes, shoes, boots, tissue paper.

The huntsman's shop. Dream of a place: hunting knives of every sort, wooden handles, extra gadgets, pouches, jerkins, belts with buckles, belts with cartridge loops and studs, flasks and hats and silver breech muskets.

Jaq forced himself on.

High up on the wall, he read the sign: *Rue d'Église*.

Jaq quickened his pace. *Pawnshop, where?*

Here.

He pressed himself close to the window. In the shadows lurked a gramophone, some skates, a mirror. *Worthless junk*.

But the other window, beyond the doorway, look. Propped up, a tray of rings. So many. How can you tell which is which?

Approaching, footsteps. Boots scuffing, the clink and rattle of soldier stuff.

The window hardly made a sound as it shattered. Inside the shop, Jaq moved fast. His eyes flitted and his heart pounded.

Another tray of rings, and another. *They all look the same*.

The footsteps are getting closer.

Crouching, Jaq turned this way and that.

Bracelets and brooches and necklaces.

Too much. There's too much.

Have to leave it. Get out.

As he hurried back round the counter, his hand caught a pile of papers. The papers sprawled on to the floor. Gleaming under them on a green baize cushion, were a diamond ring and a brooch clustered with blue stones.

A crunching behind him. The sweeping glare of a torch-beam. Framed in the broken window, a man, wearing a gendarme's cap. 'Over here, looks like a break-in.'

Jaq ducked down, backing away.

Another voice. 'Door's still locked.'

'Let's have a look inside.'

Officer Picard's boot crunched on broken glass. He swung the flashlight from side to side across the shop.

'Nothing seems to have been moved,' said the other gendarme.

'We must have surprised them.'

'Looting, at a time like this. It makes you sick.'

Picard reached down to the floor. 'Something here.'

He pushed aside the scattered papers, picked up the green baize cushion.

'What's that?' hissed the other flick. Swung his torch.

A skinny shadow burst up and over the counter, bounced off the stiff uniform of Picard, spin-twisted across the shop, and vaulted out of the window.

Jaq sprinted along the main road. Behind him clumped the gendarmes' boots. Ahead, the roadblock. *Got to chance it.* Get back to the old town.

The sentry was lolling on the wall beside the barrier, arms folded, rifle loosely slung, cigarette glowing. Looking the other way. Jaq put his head down and ran.

'Stop him!' shouted Picard.

The sentry half-turned. Jaq jumped, landed with one foot on the top of the barrier, hurdled down, stumbled. For a moment the sentry's arms were round him, fingers grasping at his shirt, but Jaq squirmed and wrenched and turned. Broke free, and past, and darted sideways, propelling himself along the wall with his hand, stumbling and sliding into the nearest alley.

Chapter Twenty-eight

They were gathered in the yard. The cows stamped. Lottie grizzling. Lise had Malcio. His ears flat, whining at the moon. Yvette put the last bag on the barrow.

'It's too much,' said Robert, trying to lift the handles.

'Take mine off,' said Grande Tante. 'We'll be back by morning.'

'All right,' said Yvette. 'Lise, give me a hand.'

They worked quickly, unloading the barrow, taking off the trunk, reloading. Yvette talked, breathless. 'We can't go to town, that's likely to be the main target. We'll have to go round the top of the Colle, and across the valley. We'll take the road where we have to, but otherwise we'll try and stick to the mule tracks.'

She tightened the straps, stood up. 'Aunt, will you go first with the cows?'

'If I have to,' grumbled Grande Tante, 'but if you ask me, it's a fool's errand, we'll be a laughing stock when they find us wet and cold on the mountain side come morning.'

Grande Tante led the way down the track. Then Lise, with Malcio. Robert struggled with the barrow. Finally Yvette, with Lottie.

Lottie whined. 'I want to stay in bed.'

'Don't we all,' agreed Grande Tante.

'Come on,' said Yvette, 'it's only five or six miles.'

Lost.

Pitch black.

The maze of alleys and steps.

Jaq crouched, panting.

He felt inside his shirt. Smiled. *Yes*. The pouch, and inside, the hard edges of the brooch, the round feel of the ring.

Which way? Up.

He slipped off his boots, tied the laces, slung them round his neck. *Now*. Slowly, carefully, he picked his way along the alley.

So quiet. Not even a dog. The cobbles slick underfoot.

Maybe the police have given up.

Steps, going up. *Try them*. Hand on the rough wall.

Above, the sky is faintly, faintly light.

A low arch above. The steps give out into another alley. Jaq edges along the alley. Feels at the walls. Looming up ahead, another wall? *Dead end*. He reaches up, to feel for a hand hold – feels at his chest the sliding, sick feeling, the pouch, dropping, loose, he grabs, but only half-catches it, something in the gloom arcs down, hits the cobbles with a sharp metallic clink – the ring, bounces, high, and clinks again, and shoots off to one side. Jaq stoops, awkward, reaches after it.

Suddenly the ring is lit up in an intense circle of white light. Jaq looks up, dazzled.

Under the arch stands Officer Picard, a flashlight in one hand, a revolver in the other.

'So,' tutted Picard, raising the revolver, 'you're just a thief, after all.'

There was a huge booming roar, which shook the whole street. It was as though a big wind blew down the alley, and grasped Jaq like a hand, and threw him sideways. Above, the sky was orange, yellow, almost as bright as day.

Lumps of concrete, bricks and metal clattered and pattered down out of the sky.

Picard, thrown to his knees by the blast, stared up, his mouth open. 'My God,' he said, 'it's started.'

The cows shouldered their way through the thick undergrowth. The branches whipped and stang. Trees loomed up round them.

'Hare-brained, stupid, waste of time,' grumbled Grande Tante, pushing ahead through the clinging foliage. 'It's too thick. I don't know where the track is.'

'Keep going,' urged Yvette, dragging Lottie by the arm. 'We should find the road in a minute.'

Lise fixed her eyes on the slow, swivelling flanks of the big cow in front. Malcio whined.

Lottie stumbled. 'Carry me,' she pleaded.

Yvette reached down, and swung Lottie up on to her hip.

'I need a rest,' complained Robert. 'My arms are nearly falling off.'

'All right,' agreed Yvette. 'Just for a –'

The sky behind flashed orange, yellow. Then the explosion. They all flinched, shrank. The rumble of the explosion still echoed round them.

'What on earth was that?' demanded Grande Tante, struggling with the cows' halters.

Malcio howled.

Lottie started snivelling.

From far below, a column of grey smoke poured up into the sky.

'I think it's the town,' said Yvette. 'They've started shelling it.'

'Come on,' said Grande Tante. 'Let's get moving.' And she swished at the flanks of the cows with her twitch. The cows lumbered forward. Lise followed, tugging Malcio.

'Faster, faster,' urged Grande Tante. And the cows lumbered into a trot, and Grande Tante, she pulled up her skirts, and hobbled along beside them. Then they were all running, stumbling, Lise tugging Malcio, Robert bumping along with the barrow, Yvette struggling on with Lottie hanging on to her neck.

They came to a gap in the trees. The road.

'Wait,' whispered Yvette. Tried to put Lottie down. Lottie clung to her neck, eyes wide open.

Yvette forced Lottie's hands loose, left and right and left and right, and right and left, Lottie clutched on again.

Yvette spoke sharply. 'I can't carry you any further.'

Lottie let go, flopped down, sitting in a loose heap, head bowed.

'Can I help?' Lise asked.

'How?' snapped Yvette.

'Listen,' Lise said, hauling Malcio closer. Her heart was bulging. Her throat was sore.

They all listened.

'Sort of crackling?' panted Grande Tante, stroking Maya's muzzle.

'It's coming from up ahead,' said Robert.

'What is it?' asked Lottie.

Yvette took a deep breath. 'I think it's machine-gun fire.'

Jaq urged himself on up the path. Somewhere, up the Colle, the Domaine. *Where is it? Which way?* No lights, only tiny flashes. Machine guns? Potch and rattle. Small arms. The roar of an engine. Coming closer. Jaq slipped into the bushes.

The motorcycle roared round the bend, and past. *French?*

Jaq's throat tightened, and he hurried on.

Which way? Where?

There was a huge puff of smoke at the other end of the

bay, and then a low boom. A moment's silence – a whistling overhead. *Artillery. Firing back at the Italians*. Far away to the east, the shell exploded with a thud.

Something on the road, by the ditch. A dark shape – shapes? Jaq crept closer, keeping close to the wall. Reached out. Something oblong, hard, an edge, a catch – he blinked. The cases lay in a mess, Robert's square one, Lise's holdall, Lottie's smaller bag. As though someone had just thrown them on the ground.

Jaq peered about. His chest tightened.

Your fault.

The words crept up into his head, like madness.

He felt at the pouch in his inside pocket. *Still there*.

Which way?

Ahead a flash, and then a whizzing, and a crash. Mortars? He crouched off the road, and along the track, up the slope.

'Move, move, move,' murmured Grande Tante, brushing at the lumbering flanks of the cows as they plodded on through the undergrowth. Lise looked back over her shoulder. Maman and Robert, struggling with the cart, one handle each. Bouncing on the cart, Lottie, clinging on, shivering, sobbing.

High above them on the mountain, the chatter of a machine gun.

Lottie wailed.

'Be quiet!' hissed Yvette.

Lottie clamped her mouth shut.

Lise looked up the slope. There was a stutter of flashes, then a rattle and pop. She ducked down, instinctively. Yvette urged her, 'Keep going, keep going.'

Lise pulled Malcio forward.

The cart wheel caught on a stone; the cart jarred and toppled. Robert swore, steadied it. Lottie sprawled half out, but clung on, keeping her mouth tight shut.

'It's no good,' said Yvette, rubbing at the blister on her palm, 'we'll have to risk it on the road.'

Jaq moved fast through the trees, above the winding road. Every few metres he stopped, peered down. *Where are they?* All around, the rattle and potch of small guns.

He crouches, panting, looking at the road below. Uneasy, shifting, squirming, shivering. *Maybe they're already safe.*

He stood up, set off – *what's that?*

Moving stealthily, a rustling below at the side of the road, a rustling and a shifting of trees and bushes, shadows. No shapes visible, but a shifting and a movement . . .

A dark shape crouches out of the bushes. Fuzzy in the dark. Jaq squinted, struggling to focus his eyes.

Soldier. And another, and another, crouching with rifles. One turns, and for a moment Jaq catches his head in silhouette against the lighter grey of the road. Helmets oval, with a dip: *French.* One of the soldiers hisses an order, and the soldiers melt back into the trees.

Jaq swallows, crouches lower, turns to slither away – but

what's that? Further along the road? Coming the other way?

Four-hundred metres away, moving carefully but quickly along the white ribbon of the road, is a small group of soldiers. Advancing, in a strange rhythmic dance, one soldier patters ahead, they spread to the road sides, then the front man waves them on, and two more men hunch their way up the road. Like some strange insect. The helmets are round like a basin, gleaming black: *Italian.*

Jaq glanced back the other way. The French soldiers have disappeared in the undergrowth, their shapes blended with the gloom of the bushes.

Ambush.

Jaq licked his lips. Shivered.

At a point halfway between the two groups of soldiers, something was standing in the middle of the road. Jaq tensed. What? He narrowed his eyes. A goat. Then the goat backed a step, as a white shape floated out of the bushes, and hovered at the roadside, looking one way, then the other. A pale, slender figure with a golden halo.

Madame.

Another, smaller figure edged out beside her. *Lise.*

Jaq bites his lip. *Get back. Get back.*

Lise reached out towards the goat. 'Who lost you?'

The goat lowered its head.

'Come on, don't be scared.'

'Leave it,' hissed Robert, 'let's keep moving.'

'Yes, come on,' called Yvette, half-turning back to the bushes.

Lise heard, but something drew her. The goat was probably one of Monsieur Angelotti's. Scared by the explosions. Had they left him? She reached out to take the dangling halter.

Jaq held his breath. *Like she's at the damn zoo.*

The Italian Blackshirts were up to the bend, their boots scuffing and clicking on the road.

Jaq stood up, shouting, waving his arms. 'Get back, get back, get back!'

There was a hiss like a rocket, and then the whole corner of the valley was lit up bright as day, but a sick, yellow, wavery light, as though the sun was tired and dying. Jaq froze, looked up. The flare dangled from the parachute, fizzing and dazzling.

Clearly etched out like toy figures were the soldiers, dark shapes against the white-grey dust of the road. Guns like sticks in their hands. The muzzles flashed. Then the echoing crack crack crack.

All around the goat, dust spurted, and a split second later a loud sharp rat-tat-tat, and the goat flinched, then shuddered, then slowly the legs crumpled and it sank to the ground.

Lise, frozen for a second, found she was running, leaping off the road, down the dusty slope.

Something whined and spat into the dust at Jaq's feet. He threw himself sideways. Another whine, another spat. Jaq rolled, glimpsed down the hill. The bushes were shaking. Lise and Madame had disappeared.

And then the flare died, and everything was dark, dark, dark: darker than it had ever been.

Jaq squirmed up the slope, away from the road.

He stopped.

Ahead there was the scuffling, tearing sound of someone forcing their way through the undergrowth.

Jaq flattened himself.

The bushes shook and parted.

A man, with a rifle. Stopped, stooped, sniffed. Jaq held his breath. In the gloom he saw a mess of silver hair, and then two bright eyes. The eyes met his. Giuseppe.

Giuseppe raised his gun to his shoulder.

Jaq pressed his face into the dirt.

There was a single potch of gunfire. Jaq raised his head.

Behind him there was a groan. Out of the bushes staggered an Italian corporal, clutching his neck. Blood was pouring over his uniform.

A strong hand grasped Jaq's arm, and pulled him to his feet.

'You all right?'

Jaq nodded.

Giuseppe's eyes darted here, there. He pointed. 'That way. Cross the road. Go!'

Chapter Twenty-nine

Lise ran.

In her mind she could still see the goat, and now as she recalled, she could see the spreading bright-red pool of blood under the animal's shaggy fur.

Run!

She tore in and out of the trees. Here the bushes were thick, like a thick hedge, catching and scratching. She wriggled and spun and pulled and pushed, eyes shut.

Maman? Robert? Where? Dare not shout out.

Are the soldiers after her? Who?

She paused, panting. *So dark.* Try to remember, where you are, where the valley is here, which way to go. Shuts her eyes. *Think, think, think.*

A sound, to her left, the road side. Lise swallows, edges away, further down the hill. The bushes cling to her.

Another sound, like an animal. Rustling, closer.

Run!

Down to the dry stream then up the far bank, up the far bank. She scrabbles in the dirt, and slips. Again, and again, her feet slipping in the dirt, and then – she sprawls, and someone's on top of her, a hand over her mouth. She tries to scream and squirms and rolls on to her back, and there he is.

'Jaq!'

They crouched together along the path.

'I don't know where the others are,' Lise whispered, breathless.

Jaq ignored her. Eyes narrow, tilting his head this way, that way, listening, sniffing. He tripped on something. The cart, lying on its side, the front wheel still slowly spinning.

Jaq moved forward into the darkness, the leaves rustling, the twigs crackling under his feet.

Something ahead. Someone? He stopped, and listened.

Breathing. Low breathing. With a choke in it. He blinked, strained his eyes. Slowly, slowly edged forwards.

A torch clicked on. Holding it, Lottie. Sat, bleary-eyed. Squatting beside her, Madame, with the revolver in her hand, pointing it straight at Jaq's heart.

They moved as fast as they could. Lise first, then Yvette, then Jaq, with Lottie hanging on his shoulders. 'Keep going downwards,' hissed Yvette. 'Find the river, follow it.'

Lise stopped. Panted. Pointed. 'Another road.'

Yvette edged carefully up the bank. Jaq knelt, Lottie's arms clinging, her breath hot on his neck.

Lise's heart was bulging up her throat. 'OK?' she whispered.

Jaq squirmed, Lottie clung tighter. Jaq nodded.

Yvette leaned back into the bushes. 'It's the Carei road.'

Jaq stood up, stumbling, hoisted Lottie higher. 'Let's go.'

Lise held up a hand. 'Something's coming.'

They cowered back into the underbrush.

Above the chatter of the machine guns came the whine and bump and whinny of an engine. Getting louder.

'Tank?' whispered Yvette.

'Truck,' breathed Jaq.

It bounced round the bend, an open-backed truck, painted dirty grey.

'Army?' Lise asked.

'No,' said Yvette, and stood up and walked out into the middle of the road.

The truck shuddered to a halt, and Old Pigache leaned out of the window. 'Come on,' he hissed. 'your auntie said I'd find you here.'

Chapter Thirty

The sky was lightening as the sun rose. Mizzi bumped her flank into Maya, then raised her head and mooed. Robert, on the ground beside them, started awake.

The smell of coffee seeped out of the metal can. The small fire crackled. In front of it, Pigache crouched, rubbing his hands, poking at the kindling. Propped against the wheel of the truck, wrapped in a dirty old blanket, Yvette and Lise, Lise's head on her mother's shoulder.

Above them, a small, pale, bleary face peered up over the side of the truck. 'Have they finished fighting yet?'

Grande Tante appeared beside Lottie. 'They've finished for now, but I reckon they'll be at it again soon.'

Lottie hugged the Marchesa doll closer to her chest.

'We're safe enough here,' coughed old Pigache.

Lise started, and woke, with a lurch of the cloak-end of a nightmare. What? The wheel was digging into her back, something hard on her cheek. She sat up.

The sky was sharp, bright blue, piercing, like toothache.

'Going to be a scorcher,' Pigache said, slopping coffee into a white enamel mug.

A red car growled round the corner and pulled up. Pierre Bernadou jumped out. 'I've got some news.'

Yvette stood up. Lise swallowed down a sick feeling, and stood up too. Pierre took hold of both Yvette's hands. 'I tried to come last night, but I couldn't get through. Are you all right?'

She nodded, and looked down at her hands, and Pierre let them go. He turned away, rubbed the back of his head, lit a cigarette. 'Paris has fallen, we've surrendered in the north.' He blew out smoke. 'The good news is, Georges is safe.' He smiled and shook his head. 'The poor fool never got into uniform.' He turned to Lise. 'And news for your thief too.'

Jaq was crouched on the edge of the ravine, looking down at the town. His shoulders squirmed, his fingers fidgeted in the dust. Lise squatted beside him.

'How goes it?' she asked.

He nodded towards the town. 'Look.'

She looked. Houses, white, red roofs, the church on the hill, the hotels, some yellow, some pink, some blue. 'What?'

He pointed. 'See that hotel? By the bridge?'

She squinted. 'It looks funny.'

And then she realised. The whole front wall had been blown out. The pillars of the main door were lopsided, the lintel skewed. An avalanche of brick and timber and plaster spewed out into the street.

The sun shone down, the birds sang. The sea was blue, and Italy faded away into the haze of the east.

Lise glanced at Jaq. He was biting his lip. His head jerked round. 'Don't keep staring at me.'

'Pierre, he brought some news. Papa's safe.'

'Good.'

'And news for you.' Her heart skipped, she tried to keep her voice casual. 'The Germans have taken Charleville.'

'I don't care.'

She leaned closer and lowered her voice. 'But all the police records there were destroyed when the Germans overran the city centre. So as far as the law's concerned, you haven't got a record any more. You're as innocent as –', she glanced round, 'one of Grande Tante's martyrs. You can make a fresh start. If you want.'

He stood up. 'Where's your ma?'

Yvette was kneeling by the fire, warming fat in a frying pan. She looked up, her green eyes dreamy, knowing.

Jaq clenched his teeth. Reached inside his shirt. 'I've got something of yours.'

She wiped her hands, stood up. Tall, slender, strong. Clumsily, he held out the jewellery pouch. Her cool, long fingers closed round it, and touched his fingers. 'Thank you,' she said. 'Thank you for looking after my things.' She smiled.

'And thank you for looking after us.'

He let go of the pouch, and it was as though he'd let go of his soul, and he was empty. If he moved, he'd disappear, or crumble into nothing.

So he stood, his eyes downcast, fixed on the ground at her feet. She reached out and touched his cheek with those same long, cool fingers, his cheek with just the first hint of stubble, and then she ducked forward, and kissed him lightly.

He turned away, his shoulders squirming, a boulder bulging in his throat, his face on fire.

No escape.

Lise was standing in front of him, dark eyes solemn. Inside her chest a rainbow was doing cartwheels in thick mud. 'Are you coming with us?'

Jaq couldn't move.

Pigache scuffed round the side of the van, coughed. 'We'd better make tracks.' He turned to Robert and Raymond. 'Lads, lead off with the cows.'

Bernard hunched up beside his father, something in his hands. Pigache coughed again, shifted his feet, addressed his words somewhere between Lise and her mother and Jaq. 'I thought I ought to tell you, by way of apology, accusing a certain party of having it when they didn't –' He pushed Bernard forward. 'What Bernard found down on the beach.'

Bernard grunted, and held up a cheap, wooden crucifix, with a dented figure hanging on by one screw.